CW00585174

Anna Kavan

Anna Kavan, née Helen Woods, was born in Cannes in 1901 and spent her childhood in Europe, the USA and Great Britain. Her life was haunted by her rich, glamorous mother, beside whom her father remains an indistinct figure. Twice married and divorced, she began writing while living with her first husband in Burma and was initially published under her married name of Helen Ferguson. Her early writing consisted of somewhat eccentric 'Home Counties' novels, but everything changed after her second marriage collapsed. In the wake of this, she suffered the first of many nervous breakdowns and was confined to a clinic in Switzerland. She emerged from her incarceration with a new name, Anna Kavan, the protagonist of her 1930 novel *Let Me Alone*, as well as an outwardly different persona and a new literary style. She suffered periodic bouts of mental illness and long-term drug addiction – she had become addicted to heroin in the 1920s and continued to use it throughout her life – and these facets of her life feature prominently in her work. She destroyed almost all of her personal correspondence and most of her diaries, therefore ensuring that she achieved her ambition to become 'one of the world's best-kept secrets'. She died in 1968 of heart failure, soon after the publication of her most celebrated work, the novel *Ice*.

I AM
LAZARUS

ANNA KAVAN

I AM
LAZARUS

With a foreword by Victoria Walker

Peter Owen
London and Chicago

PETER OWEN PUBLISHERS
81 Ridge Road, London N8 9NP

Peter Owen books are distributed in the USA and Canada by
Independent Publishers Group/Trafalgar Square
814 North Franklin Street, Chicago, IL 60610, USA

© Anna Kavan 1945
© Rhys Davies and R.B. Marriott 1978
Foreword © Victoria Walker 2013
First published in Great Britain 1945
Reprinted 1978
This Peter Owen Modern Classic edition 2013

All Rights Reserved.
No part of this publication may be reproduced
in any form or by any means without the prior
permission of the publishers.

All correspondence quoted in the Foreword is held by
the Alexander Turnbull Library, Wellington, New Zealand
(MS-Papers-7938)
© Estate of Anna Kavan 2013
Reproduced by permission of David Higham Associates

ISBN 978-0-7206-1493-0

A catalogue record for this book is available from
the British Library

Printed and bound in the UK by
CPI Group (UK) Ltd, Croydon CR0 4YY

Foreword

First published in 1945, *I Am Lazarus* was Anna Kavan's second collection of stories under her new name. Having previously published under the name Helen Ferguson, by this time she had begun using Anna Kavan (the name of one of her fictional characters) in all areas of her life. Readers familiar with her work will find echoes of the dystopian world of *Asylum Piece* and the hallucinatory, apocalyptic atmosphere of *Ice*. Written and set during the Second World War, the war not only provides a historical backdrop to the stories but shapes and saturates these narratives. On her return to England late in 1942, after more than three years travelling on five continents, Kavan was obliged to settle in London and find work. Her letters reveal that the Blitz-torn capital and the dull terror of everyday life there penetrated her self-assurance more profoundly than the far greater hazards she had risked in crossing the oceans. She writes of the relentless misery of the blackout, poor food and rationing and the atmosphere of terrible apprehension; she notes, 'O, but it's dreary here, the war and the winter, the blackout, the dismal faces, the cold, the shabbiness, the feeling of death in the air' (14 November 1943). We read these sentiments in the *Lazarus* stories, and in these fictional contexts Kavan's pacifism makes this a war without the possibility of a positive outcome. There is no right side to the conflict and no hope of victory; we see the human race destroying itself both physically and ideologically.

In 1943 Kavan worked at the Mill Hill Emergency Hospital in London, a military neurosis centre that was an outpost of the

Maudsley Hospital during the war. The patients treated at Mill Hill were soldiers suffering from 'effort syndrome', known more colloquially as 'soldiers' heart'. Their symptoms included fatigue, shortness of breath on exertion and pains in the left side of the chest; the condition had previously been believed to be a form of cardiac disorder. However, these physiological symptoms were without physical cause, and 'effort syndrome' was now identified as a psychosomatic disorder – a type of war neurosis. The early method of community therapy practised at Mill Hill offered Kavan a unique opportunity to become directly involved with treatment, and the job allowed her, for a time, to swap the role of psychiatric patient for that of psychiatric worker. Her main task was to interview patients about their history and symptoms, and her letters reveal that she felt an uncharacteristic sympathy for the men with whom she spent time.

Kavan's experiences in working at Mill Hill were clearly a strong influence on the *I Am Lazarus* stories. 'Who Has Desired the Sea', 'The Blackout' and 'Face of My People' all take a hospitalized soldier suffering from war neurosis as their protagonist, but these are not the shell-shocked figures one might expect from war literature. The trauma of battle is not the sole cause of their psychological damage – childhood experiences and social circumstance play equal parts in their distress; war exacerbates old psychological wounds. Feelings of displacement and homesickness, the awful responsibility for the lives of others and the sight of so much pain and wasted life, these more than violence and bloodshed are the precipitants of the soldiers' breakdowns. These are some of Kavan's most touching and finely rendered protagonists. Although they are unable to communicate their suffering to those around them, their emotional pain and depression are achingly palpable to the reader.

Cyril Connolly's offer of an assistant's job at the literary journal *Horizon*, which would allow her more time to write, prompted Kavan to leave Mill Hill after just four months. At *Horizon* she socialized with London's literary élite including

Connolly, Peter Watson and Arthur Koestler, although her drug-taking and psychological instability sometimes made her unpopular. She published articles and literary reviews in the journal, as well as two of the stories in this collection. In 'The Case of Bill Williams' Kavan exemplified her ease in slipping across the boundaries between fact and fiction by presenting the character of Private Bill Williams, a fictional patient in a military psychiatric hospital, and persuading the psychiatrist Maxwell Jones and the psychoanalyst Edward Glover to comment on her imaginary character. We see the subversive Bill Williams reappear here in a cameo role in the story 'Face of My People'. Kavan's interest in anarchistic politics is manifest in this article, and she mounts an attack on the normative standards of both the psychiatric profession and modern society as a whole, predicting that the fate of mankind is in peril unless 'a tonic epidemic of madness blazes across the world like a comet' (*Horizon*, No. 50, February 1944). This is Kavan's solution to the crisis of humanity – universal neurosis. Madness, for her, is not a disease but salvation, a resistance to conformity, and we see these sentiments echoed in the collection.

Kavan's critique of psychiatric confinement and treatments is clear in a number of these stories, especially those portraying the use of psychiatric drugs and prolonged narcosis, which she herself experienced. Thomas Bow, the Lazarus of the title story, has been revived from catatonia but remains institutionalized and isolated, an uncanny automaton acting out a conformity that he does not understand. Like the patients undergoing narcosis in 'Palace of Sleep', the treatment has not resurrected him to life; he is the walking dead.

Other stories locate disturbing experiences and emotional trauma outside the institution; 'All Kinds of Grief Shall Arrive' and 'A Certain Experience' evoke the Kafkaesque dystopia of *Asylum Piece*. In a world at war the layers of secrecy, bureaucracy and social control are further augmented, increasing the sense of inevitable doom and horror with which Kavan's characters live.

Many of these protagonists are foreigners, dislocated and dispossessed, literal as well as metaphorical outsiders. Mystical birds materialize at the edges of their troubled psyche; not only portentous, they are vicious agents of destruction, metaphorical incarnations of the proliferation of air power during the war. Birds are nowhere more prominent in the collection than in the Hitchcockian horror story 'The Gannets', and the image of the sacrificial child in this chilling vision recalls some of Kavan's most striking artwork. Eyeless figures in poses of execution dominate her 'dark' paintings, many of which were apparently destroyed by her executors after her death.

There is no trace in these stories of the cultural myth of the Blitz; no collective spirit, no triumph of grit and resilience, no cheery motto of 'We can take it'. Instead, Kavan's narrators are frightened and isolated figures, and her literary representations reveal the awful apprehension and emotional fragility of London's inhabitants during the Second World War. The air raids of 'Glorious Boys' and 'Our City' are the most graphic evocations of war here. In 'Glorious Boys' the narrator remembers standing in the street after a raid and feeling 'the anguish of exploded walls, burst roof, torn girders wrenching away'. In 'Our City' what is at one moment outside the black windows, far away over the city, is in the next buzzing round the narrator's head, 'scissoring through my nerves' and 'ultimately on top of me'. These nameless narrators feel the devastation wreaked on the city and its buildings as their own. Things play a prominent role in many of the *Lazarus* stories, and in the fantastic, war-ravaged world of 'Our City' they become genuine protagonists. During the raid the clock remains diligent and indefatigable, the bottles on the dressing-table snigger against one another, but the pale-blue carpet never turns a hair. Things conspire and delight in the narrator's fear, but they can also be her allies; her books are 'honourable and precious' to her, 'like members of a suicide squad who do not hesitate to engage the enormously superior enemy, life, on my behalf'. Literature weighs into the battle, a salvation not from death but from life, revealing Kavan's belief in the redemptive qualities of fiction.

Kavan's time working with soldiers suffering from 'effort syndrome' can be seen to shape the stories in ways that extend further than her representations of war-shocked men. The intimacy of psychological distress and physiological feelings that characterizes the syndrome surfaces in her representations of the effects of war throughout this collection. Kavan described in a letter to her lover Ian Hamilton her feelings on returning to Blitz-torn London with few possessions and fewer friends:

> And then the awful force of inanimate things: a broken umbrella on the steps of a blitzed house, a barrage balloon on the ground in an empty park in the rain. It's very ridiculous that those things should make you feel as if your heart were broken up in small pieces. (14 February 1943)

This letter usefully calls attention to the peculiar status of inanimate objects in Kavan's wartime London – that is, their awful force. In these stories familiar, comfortable and quotidian things become strange and absurd; their poignant incongruity skews into a complicity in the horror. Kavan's heartbreak recalls the symptoms of war neurosis in her patients – for her the evidence of war brings on the symptoms of a metaphorically broken heart, just as war brings on the psychosomatic symptoms of the same thing in 'effort syndrome'. The strange happenings in Kavan's fictional London manifest the psychological trauma of war.

Kavan's war years were scarred by bouts of ill health, depression and the loss of her son, but they were also some of her most adventurous, creatively prolific and politically engaged. In *I Am Lazarus* she offers a profound critique of social conformity and represents the experiences of those who are marginalized and dispossessed, inside asylums and out in a hostile world. In her peculiar and fantastic fictional worlds, madness and war initiate a radical dissolution of the boundaries between bodies and emotions, people and things and the city and its inhabitants. Edwin Muir best captured the essence of these stories and their power to move when he wrote that 'we do not know the world in which these things are happening, and yet we feel their truth, and feel that they are telling us something which could be told in no other way' (*Listener*, 5 April 1945).

Victoria Walker
Anna Kavan Society
2013

THE English doctor had not particularly wanted to visit the clinic. He distrusted foreigners and their ways, especially their medical ways. He distrusted anything he did not understand. In particular he distrusted this insulin shock treatment there had been such a fuss about. Why should putting imbeciles into a coma make them sane? It didn't make any sense. He did not think and he never had thought that there was a cure for an advanced dementia praecox case like young Thomas Bow.

The English doctor was not a very good doctor. He was middle-aged and frustrated and undistinguished and he would never have been consulted by the rich Mrs. Bow if she had not happened to buy a country house near the village in which he practised.

When Mrs. Bow had heard that the doctor was taking his wife for a motor tour on the Continent for their summer holiday she had suggested that he might call in to see her son if he should be any-where near the clinic. The doctor realized that a suggestion from Mrs. Bow was practically a command. No one understood better than he did the importance of keeping on the right side of a wealthy patient. Besides, it would sound well when he visited his colleagues at home after the trip. He imagined himself drinking a glass of sherry with old Leigh and casually talking about it. 'Oh yes, I had a look round the Dessones clinic when I was over there. One must keep in touch with modern developments, you know.'

The English doctor thought about these things as he walked with the superintendent in the grounds of the clinic. He also thought of the time nearly a year ago when Mrs. Bow had told him that she had decided to send her son to this continental place someone had told her about. The doctor had opposed the idea. It was a useless expense. It couldn't possibly do any good. But she was determined. Well, she had plenty of money, so what did it matter? A pretty penny it must be costing her too, he thought. The thought gratified him. He glanced at the beautifully kept gardens. The grounds were really magnificent, the watered lawns green in spite of the dry summer, every tree pruned to perfection, the borders brilliant with flowers.

Out of the blue foreign sky the sun lavishly and impartially poured itself upon the two doctors, the handsome grey-haired superintendent with his white coat, the Englishman in his hot looking tweeds.

'Wonderful place you've got here,' the visitor said in the ungracious English way that made the remark sound patronizing.

The superintendent spoke English and four other languages with complete fluency. He gracefully signified his appreciation of the other's approval. He had exactly estimated the unimportance of his companion but it was his policy to treat everyone with polite attention. This was one of the secrets of his success.

'We're very proud of Mr. Bow,' he said. 'He's an outstanding example of the success of the treatment. He responded wonderfully well from the start and I consider him a quite remarkable cure. In a few months he should be well enough to go home. We're just keeping him under observation now.'

The English doctor began for the first time to think about Thomas Bow whom he was to see in a few moments and whom he had last seen hopelessly insane. He wondered how he would see him to-day. They walked on. Behind stood the big main building, white like a smart hotel with striped awnings and window boxes bright with scarlet geraniums. In front were the workrooms, the studios, where the patients were employed at various handicrafts.

The superintendent opened the door of a well-lighted room with a long table at which men and women were working. The sun came through the windows and shone on their hands moving over the table. Some of them were talking. There was a little froth of talk in the room which bubbled away into nothingness as the door opened. A man in an overall was in charge. He had a good-humoured face with freckles across his cheeks. He stood behind one of the patients showing him what to do. The different pairs of hands, large and small, rose and fell over the table.

'Quite a hive of industry, you see.' The superintendent was bland.

The Englishman looked uneasily at the faces and at the hands which seemed to be rising and falling of their own volition in the banded sunshine above the table.

The superintendent stepped up to the table.

'Good morning, Mr. Bow. I've brought you a visitor.'

A young man of about twenty-two, very neatly dressed in a grey suit, was sitting there with a strip of leather held in his hands. He had a pale, full, rather nice-looking face and dark hair brushed very smooth. His nose was aristocratic. He was well-built, on the big side; a little fleshy, perhaps. He looked squarely at the two doctors out of flat hazel eyes.

'You remember me, don't you?' the English visitor said, giving his name.

He held out his hand and after a slight pause the other man put down the piece of leather and shook the hand. He did not smile.

'Glad to see you looking so fit,' said the doctor, bringing into action his falsely hearty professional tone. He unobtrusively scrutinized the young man who sat stiffly correct in his place at the sunny table, holding the strip of leather again.

'What are you making?' the superintendent asked him.

'A belt,' said the patient, and smiled.

He liked making the belt and so it pleased him to have someone notice it and he smiled.

'It's pigskin,' he explained. He liked speaking about the belt.

'Very nice,' the English doctor said, not quite at ease.

'Yes,' Thomas Bow said. 'I made another before but it was too narrow. This is a much better one.'

He looked satisfied, sure of being on safe ground. The superintendent patted his shoulder, a few more remarks were exchanged, and the doctors went out again.

'I should never have believed it possible,' the Englishman said with emphasis and repressed indignation. 'Never.'

He felt disapproving and indignant and uncomfortable without quite knowing why. Of course, the boy looks normal enough, he said to himself. He seems quiet and self-controlled. But there must be a catch in it somewhere. You can't go against nature like that.

It just isn't possible. He thought uneasily of the young inexpressive face and the curious flat look of the eyes.

In the workroom the unsustained talk started again like the twitter of nervous birds in an aviary. Mr. Bow took no notice. He spoke to no one and nobody spoke to him. He methodically went on sewing the pigskin belt with steady, regular movements of his soft hands. It was satisfactory. What had he to do with talking? All around the table were different coloured shapes whose mouths opened and closed and emitted sounds that meant nothing to him. He did not mind either the shapes or the sounds. They were part of the familiar atmosphere of the workroom where he felt comfortable and at ease.

A buzzer set in the wall made a noise like an angry wasp. The patients rose from the table and went away, some singly, some in small groups. Now it was quiet in the workroom. The man in the overall started tidying up. He moved round the table arranging things neatly and putting other things away on the shelves.

Mr. Bow sat on in his place sewing the pigskin belt. He did not want to go out of the workroom where he felt confident and secure. Outside things were different.

The freckled man left him in peace until the whole room was tidy. Then he came up and touched his arm. 'Time to go to déjeuner, Monsieur Bow.' He put out his strong brown hand for the belt and the white hands of Mr. Bow reluctantly yielded it up.

'See, I take great care of it for you,' the man said kindly. He rolled the belt and wrapped it in a clean cloth and put it away in a special place at the back of one of the shelves.

Thomas Bow watched carefully. When he was sure that the belt was finally and safely disposed of he went out of the workroom. The other man followed him out and shut the door and locked it and dropped the key into his pocket and walked quickly away to his lunch.

Mr. Bow sauntered slowly in a different direction, towards the main building. Once or twice he glanced back at the workroom. Each time he saw the door still blankly closed against him and he sighed. He walked rather stiffly on a path that crossed a park-like expanse of ground. The grass here had not been cut but grew up tall between clumps of fine trees. Moon daisies grew in the grass. They had yellow eyes that squinted craftily through the grass.

The grass grew up tall and feathery. The grasses whispered together and turned their heads in the breeze. Mr. Bow touched the heads of the grasses with his soft fingers. The grasses responded felinely; like thin sensitive cats they arched themselves to receive the caress of his finger-tips. The young man stood still and picked one of the grasses and brushed it against his cheek. It touched his skin lightly, prickingly, like the electrified fur of a cat in a thunderstorm. He picked several more grasses.

Suddenly he was aware of a presence. The gym mistress cycling along the path had approached noiselessly. She skipped neatly off her bicycle. Like everyone else employed in the clinic she was big and healthy and strong. The sun-bleached hairs on her muscular brown arms glittered like gold. At the gymnastic class she often spoke sharply to Mr. Bow because he was clumsy and slow. Now, however, she spoke in a friendly way.

'Why, Mr. Bow, what are you doing with those?'

The young man laboriously assembled words in his head. He wished to explain that the grasses turned into soft-furred cats and arched their backs under his hand.

The gym mistress did not listen to what he was trying to say. It was not the fashion at the clinic to listen to what patients said. There was not enough time. Instead, she put out her hand. Steadying the bicycle with her left hand, she stretched out her right and took the grasses away from Thomas Bow and threw them down on the path. A few seeds had stuck to his jacket and she brushed them off briskly.

'You don't want those,' she said. 'Nobody picks grass. We could pick some flowers though, if you like.' She reached down for a handful of moon daisies and offered them to him. 'There, aren't they pretty?' She was very good-natured about it.

Mr. Bow unwillingly accepted the flowers.

'Come on,' she said. 'You'll be late for lunch if you don't hurry.' She walked strongly beside him wheeling the bicycle. Some part of the mechanism accompanied them with a soft whirring noise.

The young man glanced with dislike at the daisies he carried. Their yellow eyes had a base and knowing expression. When the gym mistress was not looking he dropped them and trod on them with his brown shoe.

Inside the clinic he went into the washroom. Several coats hung on the wall. Thomas Bow avoided the wash-basins nearest the coats. The hanging shapes filled him with deep suspicion. He watched them out of the ends of his eyes to make sure they did not get up to anything while he was washing his hands. Just as he was ready to go someone else came into the cloakroom, an Italian two or three years younger than he. He frowned and hurried towards the door. He did not like Sanguinelli who had eyes like black minnows that darted about in his face. Sanguinelli's face was never at rest; the muscles jumped and twitched like mice caught in traps under the skin.

'Goo-ood morn-eeng,' he said. He grinned. He only knew a few English words.

The other man did not answer but hastily opened the door. The Italian arrested him with a shrill whistle and pointed mockingly towards the Englishman's lower middle. Mr. Bow looked down guiltily. Sometimes he forgot to do up his fly buttons and when this happened one of the doctors would reprimand him. The buttons were fastened now. Sanguinelli let out a hoot of derision.

In the passage a nurse was going towards the door that led to the staff-rooms. The door-female situation was one with which Thomas Bow was quite familiar. The doctors had impressed upon him what he must do whenever it presented itself. He stepped forward politely and opened the door. He smiled. It pleased him that he knew so well what to do. The nurse smiled back. She thanked him and said how well he was looking. Then she went through the door and shut it behind her.

'Flirting with Mr. Bow?' said her friend who was passing by.

'I'm sorry for him,' said the nurse. 'He does try so hard to do what he's told. He's a nice-looking boy, too. It's a shame.'

12

'He gives me the creeps,' said the other girl. 'Like an automaton walking about. Like a robot. When you think what he was like when he first came it's uncanny. And he always looks so worried. I believe he'd have been happier left as he was. What d'you suppose goes on inside his head?'

'Heaven knows,' said her friend.

Mr. Bow was sorry that there were no more doors which he could open for ladies to pass through. He went into the hall where most of the patients were already assembled. He sat down on a hard chair in the background. He was relieved because nobody spoke to him. There was the same sort of noise here as there had been in the workroom, the sort of sporadic twittering that might come from a collection of timid cage-birds. The young man looked round cautiously. The pretty dresses of the women gave him pleasure but he was not at ease. At any moment something might pounce on him, something for which he did not have the formula. He waited tensely, on enemy ground.

The gong sounded, the doctor on duty appeared, and the patients flocked after him into the dining-hall. The table places were altered at every meal and each patient's place was marked with a card on which was written his name. The waiters, like well-trained sheep-dogs, skilfully manœuvred the patients towards their chairs. Mr. Bow was glad to find that he was not to sit beside one of the so-called hostesses who were spaced round the big table to watch what went on. The patients stood at their places, waiting for the doctor to sit down. The doctor glanced round to make sure that everybody had found the right seat. Then he sat down. It was the signal. The room was full of loud scrapings as the patients pulled back their chairs.

Mr. Bow prepared to sit down with the rest but there was an obstruction; something impeded him. Sanguinelli had slipped quick as an eel between him and his chair. The Italian's eyes, full of malice, writhed like insane tadpoles from side to side.

'Excuse — my place.' He pointed towards the name card with a thin yellow finger.

'No,' said Thomas Bow, frowning. He was angry. He was tormented and persecuted and he would not endure it. He snatched at the back of the chair but Sanguinelli was seated in it already. Everyone was sitting down now except the waiters and Mr. Bow.

A hostess two places away took charge of the situation. Her hair went in hard, regular waves.

'This is your seat here, Mr. Bow,' she said amicably. There was a chair empty beside her.

'No,' said the Englishman slowly. 'No.' He frowned deeply. 'My card is here.'

The Italian burst out laughing. He triumphantly displayed the card in front of him on which was written the name Sanguinelli. The hostess looked down and saw that the card next to her was indeed the name card of Thomas Bow.

'Come along, Mr. Bow. You've made a mistake,' she said in a firmer tone.

The young man recognized the firmness that was in her voice. He moved obediently and sat down in the empty chair and spread his table napkin widely over his knees as he had been shown how to do. He ate what was put before him, looking carefully at his neighbours to make sure that he used the same knives and forks as they did. All the time he was eating he felt angry and sad and confused. Something had happened which he did not understand. The card with his name had been there, he had seen it distinctly, but when he looked at it again Sanguinelli's name had appeared. Sanguinelli had triumphed over him in front of the whole room and it was unfair. He had heard the laughter go round the table. His heart was full of sorrow and shame. From time to time the Italian boy leaned forward and grinned at him from the stolen place, triumphant because no one had seen him exchange the cards.

After lunch the patients went out into the grounds. Games were organized. Mr. Bow was directed to take part in the simplest game which consisted in throwing large wooden balls at a smaller ball some distance off. Mr. Bow did not understand the game. He did not understand why some of the balls were brown and some black or why one player threw before another. He stood with the large shiny ball in his hand, waiting till he should be told to throw. He was not thinking about the game. He was thinking about the pig-skin belt he was making. It seemed to him that the belt was his friend. Only the feel of the cool leather could assuage the hurt and the anger inside his heart.

The time came for him to make his throw. He held the ball cupped in his hand as he saw the other players do. He aimed conscientiously at the little ball lying out on the grass but his ball disobeyed him and flew far beyond. There was laughter. 'Champion! Champion!' jeered the Italian voice.

Thomas Bow wandered away from the game. No one noticed him going. He wandered towards the workroom. He held out his hands to the grasses, but now they did not caress his skin like soft fur but pricked sharp as needles. As he walked he hoped very much that the workroom door would be open. It was shut, and blinds were drawn over the windows.

The young man sat down on the step in front of the workroom door. He looked bewildered and worried and very sad. He did not know what to do. It troubled him that the belt was locked away in there. He felt the belt lonely for him as he was for it. He glanced up. A cloud had passed over the sun. He would have liked to share his worry with the cloud but the cloud would not stay. He sat disconsolate on the step staring flatly ahead.

Presently he heard voices and two men came round the corner of the building. One of them was a man who visited the clinic periodically to do X-ray work. The other was a doctor with black hair and a bluish chin. Mr. Bow was afraid of the doctor who for many months had put him into a hideous sleep with his poisoned needle.

'Hullo, what are you doing here?' the radiologist asked.

'I came for my belt,' he answered. He stood up.

He was afraid of the doctor and wanted to get away in case he should be trapped and put back again into the nightmare sleep.

'Your belt?' The other man did not understand.

'He's doing leather work at occupational therapy. I suppose he's making a belt,' the doctor explained. He came up to the patient. 'Don't you know that the workroom's closed in the afternoon?' he

15

said to him. 'It's recreation time now. Get off and join the others.'
He gave him a friendly push. Mr. Bow started back in alarm.

'I only wanted my belt,' he said, starting to move away.

The other two watched him go.

'He doesn't know how lucky he is,' said the dark doctor. 'We've
pulled him back literally from a living death. That's the sort of
thing that encourages one in this work.'

Mr. Bow walked carefully in the sunshine. He did not know
how lucky he was and perhaps that was rather lucky as well.

PALACE OF SLEEP

THE wind 'was blowing like mad in the hospital garden. It seemed to know that it was near a mental hospital, and was showing off some crazy tricks of its own, pouncing first one way and then another, and then apparently in all directions at once. The mad wind sprang out with a bellow from behind a corner of the nurses' quarters, immediately tearing round the back of the building to meet itself half-way along the front in a double blast that nearly snatched the cap from the head of a sister hurrying towards the entrance. With a clash and a clatter the door swung to admit her indignant figure huddled in its blue cloak. The wind came in too with a malicious gusto that died drearily in the recesses of the hall where the two doctors were talking.

The physician in charge glanced round as if he resented the unceremonious way the wind burst into his hospital. He was a man of about sixty-five, with a red, cheerful face and white hair. Magnanimously passing over the wind's interruption, he went on with the story he was telling.

'When I went in next morning she was trying to tear up the sheet. So I said to her in a quiet, friendly way, "Don't you think that's rather a silly thing to do?" And she answered me back as quick as lightning, "If I can't do silly things here, I'd like to know where I can do them".' The red face creased into a net of jovial lines, the broad shoulders shook with laughter. 'Pretty smart, wasn't it?'

The young doctor echoed the laugh politely. He was a visitor from the north who was being shown round the hospital. Himself a reticent man, he wished that the superintendent were a little less genial and expansive. So much good-humour aroused in him some disquietude, some slight distrust. He turned his lean, sensitive face, and his eyes rested reflectively on the other for a moment. What they saw was not altogether reassuring. There was something which they found faintly suspect about the appearance of the elderly man. His hair was too white, his face was too genial, his expression was too optimistic. He looked more like a country parson than a psychiatrist.

The visitor looked at his watch and said tentatively, 'I'm afraid I haven't much time left. I think you were going to show me the paying block — ?'

'Yes, yes. The paying block. You must certainly see that before you go. We're very proud of our private wards.'

The swing doors clashed behind the two men, who lowered their heads against the attack of the wind. The wind leaped madly upon them, with malice, with joy, as they walked on the covered way that crossed the impersonal garden. In the empty flower-beds the earth lay saturated and black, the wintry-looking, acid-green grass rippled under the wind, the bare trees lashed their branches complainingly.

The two doctors walked briskly along side by side, the one tall, contemplative, reserved, turned in upon himself against the onslaught of wind, the other with white hair blowing about and a look of determined good-nature which seemed to set the seal of his approval upon the rough weather.

The long brick building felt quiet as a vacuum after the windy tumult outside. The superintendent paused for a moment inside the door, smoothing his beautiful white hair with his fingers. He was slightly breathless.

'Welcome to the palace of sleep,' he said with his cheerful smile, speaking and smiling partly for the benefit of a young nurse who was passing by. 'All the patients in this wing are having partial or prolonged narcosis,' he went on in a more confidential tone as the girl disappeared through one of the many doors.

The wide corridor was coldly and antiseptically white, with a row of doors on the left and windows on the opposite side. The windows were high and barred, and admitted a discouraging light that gleamed bluishly on the white distemper like a reflection of snow. Some grey rubber composition which deadened sound covered the floor. A hand-rail ran along the wall under the high windows.

One of the doors further down the corridor opened, and a nurse emerged, supporting a woman in a red dressing-gown. The patient swayed and staggered in spite of the firm grip that guided her hand to the rail. Her head swung loosely from side to side, her wide-open eyes, at once distracted and dull like the eyes of a drunken person, stared out of her pale face, curiously puffy and smooth under dark hair projecting in harsh, disorderly elf-locks. Her feet, clumsy and uncontrolled in their woollen slippers, tripped over the hem of her long nightdress and threw her entire weight on the nurse's supporting arm.

'Hold up, Topsy,' the probationer said, in a tolerant, indifferent voice just perceptibly tinged with impatience, speaking as if to an awkward child. She hoisted her companion upright, and the pair continued their laborious progress towards the bathroom, the sick woman stumbling and reeling, and gazing desperately, blankly ahead, the nurse watchful, abstracted, and humming a dance tune under her breath.

'That patient will finish her treatment in another day or two,' the physician-in-charge told the visitor. 'Of course, she won't remember anything that's happened to her during the period of narcosis. She's practically unconscious now, although she can manage to walk after a fashion.'

He continued to discuss technicalities as they moved together along the corridor. The young man listened and answered somewhat mechanically, his eyes troubled, disturbed by what they had seen.

A door opened as the two doctors were passing it, and the red-faced senior paused to speak to the nurse who was coming out, holding an enamel tray covered with a cloth from beneath which emanated the nauseous stench of paraldehyde. He noticed the other man's instinctive recoil, and his face wrinkled into its jolly folds.

'Don't you like our local perfume, then? We're so used to the smell of P.R. here that we hardly notice it. Some of the patients say they actually get to like it in time.'

They went into the room, which was heavy with the same sickening odour. Under the white bedspread pulled straight and symmetrical, like the covering of a bier, a young woman was lying quite motionless with closed eyes. Her fair hair was spread on the pillow, her pale face was absolutely lifeless, void, with the peculiar glazed smoothness and eye-sockets darkly circled. The superintendent stood at the bedside looking down at this shape which already seemed to have forfeited humanity and given itself over prematurely to death. His face wore a complacent expression, gratified, approving; the look of a man well satisfied with his work.

'She won't move now for eight hours, and then she'll come round enough to be washed and fed, and then we'll send her off for another eight-hour snooze.'

The visitor had come close to the bed and was also looking down at its occupant. The vague distress accumulating in his mind crystallized for some reason about this inanimate form which seemed, to his stimulated sensibilities, to be surrounded by an aura of inexpressible suffering.

'I don't know that I altogether approve of such drastic treatment for psycho-neurotics,' he was beginning: when suddenly a tremor disturbed the immobility of the anonymous face, the eyelids quivered under their load of shadows. The man watched, fascinated, almost appalled, as, slowly, with intolerable, incalculable effort, the drugged eyes opened and stared straight into his. Was it imagination, or did he perceive in their clouded greyness a look of terror, of wild supplication, of frantic, abysmal appeal?

'She's not conscious, of course,' the superintendent remarked in his benevolent voice. 'That opening of the eyes is purely a reflex. She can't really see us or hear anything we say.'

Smiling, white-headed like a clergyman, he turned and walked across to the open door. The other doctor hesitated for a few seconds in the ill-smelling room, looking down at the patient, held by an obscure reluctance to withdraw his gaze from those unclear eyes. And when he finally moved away he felt uneasy and almost ashamed, and wished that he had not come to visit the hospital.

WHO HAS DESIRED THE SEA

THE late autumn sun came into the ward about two in the afternoon. There wasn't much strength in the sun which was slow in creeping round the edge of the blackout curtains so that it took a long time to reach the bed by the window.

He lay on the bed fully dressed and watched the sun clamber feebly from one empty bed to another all down the ward, rasping the folded dark army blankets with bristles of light. When it had investigated each iron bedstead the sun slipped down and stretched itself on the floor. The floor was polished and shiny, but where the sun lay a film of dust was revealed. Bars of shadow crossed the pale sun on the floor because of the paper strips pasted over the window. He noticed, as he had noticed on previous afternoons, how the horizontal lines looked like the shadows of prison bars. The association was vaguely unpleasant, and a vague uneasiness disturbed his preoccupation. There was no sense in the paper, anyhow, he thought. It wouldn't prevent the glass splintering if a bomb dropped anywhere near.

He turned his head to the window and the uneasiness disappeared. On the window itself the paper strips were translucent and honey coloured and no longer suggestive of prison bars.

Outside the window he could see the park with trees and grass and a drive curving through. There was a white board shaped like an arrow at the edge of the drive, pointing to the hospital with the words Neurosis Centre painted on it. The tall trees were practically leafless and their black branches swayed gravely and delicately in the wind. The short grass underneath was patched with tarnished brown-gold by the fallen leaves. In summer it would be an agreeable English scene; but now the dying autumnal leaves and the sea wind gave it some desolation.

The man on the bed knew that he ought to be with the other patients, many of whom were walking about outside, their bright

21

hospital trouser-legs showing under their khaki greatcoats. He ought to get up and put on his own overcoat which hung neatly on the hook by his bed, folded in the regulation way with the buttons fastened. He knew this was what he should do. But the knowledge had no relevance. It did not seem to apply directly to him. Something like glass came in between, dividing him from it. He lay quietly looking out of the window.

It was pass day, the day visitors were allowed, and some of the soldiers out there had civilians with them, friends and relatives with whom they were going out for the afternoon. Some couples walked arm-in-arm, and there were a few family groups with children scuffing their feet through the fallen leaves. Most of those who had no visitors stepped out briskly towards the road leading to the shops and the cinema. Only here and there an isolated patient walked slowly, with bent head, looking down on the ground, or wandered aimlessly on the grass as if he did not notice where he was going.

Before the eyes of the man in the ward the scattered figures outside moved in a pattern as remotely impersonal as that of the weaving branches or the seagulls circling against the sky.

He saw these things with his blue, away-looking eyes, but he was not attending to them. He was looking for something, or rather someone, quite different: he was looking for a young man with thick brown awkward hair and a small scar on his cheek. For a long time he had been looking for this young man. It was absolutely necessary that he should find him. The man on the bed did not know how it was that he, whose life had become a lonely uncertainty, was so certain of this one thing. He did not at all understand it, but he did not question it either. He only knew with complete conviction that it was essential to him that this man should be found. Then, and not till then, he himself would be able to get outside the glass.

The sun was crawling weakly across the ward. The man stretched out and held his hand in the sun. He saw the sunshine on the back of his brown strong-fingered hand and felt the faint warmth. He felt the sunshine and saw it, but it was beyond the glass, it was not touching him really. After a moment he put his hand down again on the blanket beside him. He did not feel disappointed or troubled about the glass. He was used to it. It was queer how you got used to things, even to living inside a glass cell.

A picture of a clock drifted in front of him. It was an electric clock that had belonged to one of his aunts, it was made of brass with all its works showing, a skeleton of a clock inside a glass dome, and it never required winding. When he was a small boy there had seemed to him to be something horrific and fascinating and pathetic about the sight of the pendulum frantically swinging, swinging, swinging, perpetually exposed and driven in that transparent tomb.

A gust of wind rattled the window and blew the clock thousands of miles and days back to its mantelpiece. The man on the bed listened for the sound of waves in the wind. Although the sea was a good distance off it was possible sometimes to hear the waves break on the rocky shore. Now, as on every occasion when he was aware of the sea, a vague disquietude, restlessness, creased his forehead in anxious lines.

Now he was not able to attend to his watching, was the fear behind the anxiety. Now if the young man came near he might not be aware. The sea-sound was a distraction, interrupting his vigil.

The wind died down again and the noise of the waves was no longer distinguishable. With the patients all out on passes the hospital seemed unnaturally still. The murmurous confusion of steps and voices, the opening and closing doors which normally went unnoticed became in absence obtrusive.

Without moving his body the man turned his head from the window and looked down the empty ward. The sun had now reached the wainscot and was starting to pull itself up the wall. Soon it would catch his greatcoat and mount above it and move on up to the ceiling. Then it would go altogether and leave the ward to the strengthening shadows. But before that happened he himself would be gone. There was something which had to be done. Something immensely difficult that had to be done by him while the afternoon sun still shone. It was something he would not be able

23

to do. It was too difficult. It was impossible. But it was required of him. He would be obliged to attempt this impossible thing. He would not be allowed to evade the foredoomed attempt. They would come to the ward and fetch him away to make it.

So for these last few minutes he must wait with his whole attention for the young man with the thick untidy hair and the little scar. So he must hope that his twelfth-hour arrival would make everything plausible. Since the sea was quiet he had no more anxiety, and with the anxiety and the restlessness gone all that he felt was a great pre-occupation and longing that the young man should appear. From the effort he would soon have to make he was now dissociated. For a moment it had seemed urgent; but now the glass shut it off. It was strange how dim and unurgent the glass made it.

If only he would come now, the man thought. He was looking along the length of the ward, and watching the door. He always felt that the young man with the scar was more likely to come when there was no one about. Maybe he had something private to say, and that was why he would come when things were quiet. Well, the place was deserted enough now.

But then, inside the glass, the pendulum began madly swinging, swinging, making him feel confused. Pictures and confusion crowded inside the glass.

Now in the distance he saw the beach at Mairangi and the young man was standing there very tanned in his bathing slips and that was the small scar on his cheek that he had got from the oyster shell on the rock swimming under water when he was eight years old. That was one of the things he was seeing, with, in the background, Cape Promise and all the islands, the Sugar Loaf and The Noises, the little ones where the penguins went, and the one which was an extinct volcano. It was the strong southern sun that made the wattle burn like a yellow fire all along the creek. In Mairangi at Christmas time the sun was so strong it hurt your eyes for the first few seconds when you came out of the bach in the morning and ran down the beach to swim. That was the place where they dragged the boat over the warm sand, shells sharply warm on the foot soles, and where they had those great fishing trips out to the Barrier, the water as smooth and solid to look at as kauri gum and as blue as sapphires, and he remembered the clean splashless opening of the water as you dived into it like a knife.

But then the water was piled-up and ugly, another colour, another ocean, and that was another thing in the sky he was seeing and Shorty asking him if it were an F.W. and he looking up at it over the gun and saying, No, that's one of the escort planes. We're not in the range of the F.W.s yet. And Shorty repeating to the boys on the gun, No, it's one of ours. We're not in the range yet, and the others all saying, Must be one of the escorts. But it was a Focke Wulfe all right swooping over that evil water and it delivered them to it when the tanker's deck twisted, splintered and pulped and exploded in flame, and he remembered how the black water towered up and then the thousand-ton icy weight of it smashing down on them like a whale, the freezing, murderous bastard.

And now suddenly there was nothing but the skeleton in the transparent cell, brass midriff and spine, wheels and frangible springs, the hollow man, bloodless, heartless, headless; only the crazy pendulum swinging in place of head.

'Why are you up here? Don't you feel well?' the nurse said, coming into the ward.

'I'm all right,' he said. He looked at her and was glad because it was this nurse who had come for him, the pretty fair one, who would not make a fuss or ask too many questions.

'You haven't forgotten you've got a visitor, have you?' she said. 'You surely haven't forgotten about your fiancée coming? She's downstairs now and you ought to have been there to meet her. Did you forget to-day was visiting day?'

So, he thought, here it is: it's come now, the time when I have to do the impossible thing. And for a second he felt sick inside, but that passed, and he was behind the glass and feeling nothing at all.

'No, I hadn't forgotten,' he said.

He swung his legs off the bed and stood up tall and lean, and unhooked his coat while the nurse straightened the pillow and then came with him down the ward and waited while he held his comb under the tap at the wash-basin and tugged at the unmanageable brown hair that never would lie flat whatever he did to it with water or brilliantine.

He saw the nurse watching, and said, 'This is a kind of experiment, isn't it? To see how I get on with Nora, I mean.'

'Doctor thinks it will do you good to see her,' she said. 'That's why he told her she could come down from London to-day. It's not going to be very easy for her, you know. She's been awfully worried about you. It's up to you to show her that you're going to be quite all right.'

'Yes,' he answered, out of the glass.

They were downstairs now at the door of the waiting-room. The nurse opened the door and stepped back and he went into the room which was empty except for the girl standing close to the window; quick-smiling face and tapping heels, he watched her come quickly towards him now. Again he felt hollow sick because of the hopeless attempt, the effort which had to be made, thinking inside himself, Do I have to do this? Is it absolutely necessary to try this impossible thing? But then it passed, he felt her breath and her light kiss on his ·cheek, it was over, he was in his glass cell and it seemed quiet there and he felt nothing at all.

'It's a lovely afternoon,' the girl said presently. 'Shall we go for a walk?'

'All right.'

She was nervous, not knowing how to begin knowing him again, and, remembering his loose colonial stride and how he liked being out in the open places, she walked with him away from the town and the cinema where she would have felt at home.

She's a sweet girl really, he thought with a vague pang that was gone almost before he felt it at all. It was not her fault that he could not even feel sorry because she had come to him when he was no longer there. She was not in the least to blame. How could she know that he was a hollow thing; only wheels and a pendulum working inside a case? Because he had not found the young man with the scarred cheek he could not come to her through the glass.

She was talking to him as they walked in the thin sunshine beyond the hospital grounds. The sun was getting very low and the sea-

26

gulls were flying low over the downs where they walked. He looked at her face between him and the sky. She was walking with her head turned to him and the sinking sun shone on her pleasantly powdered face and he could see that she was trying hard to make contact with him. He heard the sea make a noise just over the rise of the hill.

'No further,' he said, standing still. 'I don't want to go on any further.'

She looked at him with surprise and said, 'Don't you want to look at the sea? Let's just walk up to the top where we can see it now that we're here. It's quite close now.'

He felt the bad feeling come on him again, but this time there was no sickness, only a sudden sinking and emptiness, as when a small ship lurches and rolls suddenly, so that he waited for the crash and slither of loose objects falling: but there was only the wind and the gulls and the waves breaking below the edge of the hill. It passed, and he started to walk on again up the slope, because it did not matter really. Nothing mattered, he thought, because nothing could reach him while he was inside the glass.

'All right,' he said. 'Let's go and look at the sea.'

And really when he saw it it did not matter: it was quite easy to look at the agitated empty pale sea that was faintly touched with lilac feathers under the sunset sky. Except that he would rather not have seen the breaking waves on the rocks at the foot of the cliff. It was quite a high cliff to which the track had led them over the downs. The girl was looking out to sea and smiling with the wind blowing back the short bits of hair round her face.

'It's fine up here, isn't it?' she said to him.

'No,' he said, 'it's the wrong sea.'

He saw the bewilderment and distress and incomprehension come instead of the smile on her face because of what he had said; and he thought that he ought to try and explain something, but it was impossible because there was nothing but the swinging pendulum with which to explain.

And at the same time he saw on sunnier cliffs barelegged girls, perhaps his sisters, riding barebacked on ponies with rough manes

27

flying, he saw the bleached gilt hairs on the brown girls' legs and heard girls' high voices calling and laughing often.

'You've always been mad on the sea,' a girl's voice was saying.

Yes, the sea was the one thing he had always been crazy about. But what had become of those other oceans? What had become of the sapphire blue deep water, the quick, clear small waves on the beaches, the purple submerged peninsulas of the reefs? Now he remembered the steady smooth rush of the sailing boat through blue sunlit water and the satisfactory slap of water on the sides of the boat. He remembered the huge seas marching past the tanker, huge and heavy and whale coloured, marching in manic persistence, the staggering deck, the water bursting endlessly over the catwalk. And for a second he remembered the time on the gun when they brought the plane down at sunrise, and for a second he was that young gunner triumphant and in his glory, the sea lunging pink-stained into oblivion past the gun sights. Then he remembered the horror that came later, the freezing, strangling, devilish masses of water, the horror of blazing oil on the water and Shorty screaming out of the flaming water. Then the cold blankness settled again and he could not remember whether he had known these things or what had become of them.

Now it was this town girl he had met on leave in the city to whom he had to attend. She was a good-looking girl; and perhaps before the glass closed round him he had felt something for her, but now there was just this impossible thing, this effort he could not make. He knew he ought to explain something. She was trying to be sweet and kind to him. But he knew he could never do the impossible thing. And just then it occurred to him that he was shaking under his khaki coat.

'What is it, Lennie?' she asked him.

'Nothing,' he said. 'It's cold standing around. Let's walk into town and get tea there. Let's get away from the sea.'

'Don't you like the sea any more?' she asked. She was looking at him walking away from the cliff, and biting her lip.

'No,' said the man. 'I don't think so. I think I hate it.'

But then, feeling the hollow, vague coldness inside the glass,

28

and going away from the sea, there was nothing at all left and nothing mattered at all.

'I don't feel anything about it,' he said. 'I don't feel anything about anything.'

On the way to the town she took his arm and they walked like that for a bit while he thought of the effort which he was required to make. He had known all the time he would not be able to make it. He knew that he had to do this tremendous thing and he wanted to do it and it was his duty to do it; but he knew that it was impossible, that he would never make the attempt now, and soon she unlinked her arm and began telling him about a picture with Spencer Tracy.

In the tea place where they sat down together it was half dark already and lamps were lighted. Drinking strong tea, with no anxiety left except the ache of the unmade and abandoned effort, the girl pouring the tea, the warmth of it spreading through him, he could feel the beginning of comfort after the dusk and the sea wind. While the waitress fastened the blackout they drank and just as the blackout was fixed and it was impossible to see out any longer, something thundered outside with a noise like a heavy sea and the man started and slopped his tea in the saucer.

'The buses stop just outside here,' the girl said. 'It's the market place and they all stop here.'

'What a filthy row,' he said, feeling the evil sickness on him again, knowing that he was shaking again under his coat. So this was how he lived now, getting jittery because a bus pulled up near. Well, he was not going on like that. It was not good enough. The one person who could help him had not appeared. He probably never would. But there must be some other way. He knew that there was another way although for the moment he couldn't think what it was. Soon it would come back to him, in a minute he would remember the way out, the way where he was going.

'Are you feeling all right?' the girl said. She had put her arms on the table and was leaning towards him.

'Of course.'

'Why don't you eat your cake?'

'I'm going to.'

The cake was too dry. He had to hold it in his mouth after he'd chewed it and then by taking a gulp of tea he was just able to wash it down without retching.

He put the cup carefully back on the saucer so that it didn't rattle. The girl touched his hand with her fingers.

'Don't you like me any more either?' she said.

'I can't explain,' he said. 'I can't help it.'

The sickness had come up in his throat now and his lungs, and he could feel it strangling him and he was drowning again in the four-mile-deep icy horror of sickness or water. He looked at the girl and saw that she was crying.

'It's no good. I can't do it,' he said.

Then he pushed back his chair and stood up quickly because, just then, he saw the young man's face in a mirror up on the wall, he saw the thick wind-ruffled hair and the little scar on the cheekbone. The face moved in the mirror and when he looked round he could not see it anywhere in the room, and when he wanted to call out the sickness choked him, and now he tried to fight off the icy sickness, but like whales the waves of it fell on him till he was pounded and drowned, and while he froze suffocating and could not move or breathe, he heard the girl say, 'Where are you going?' and then he was able to move suddenly, and he got out of the tea-room.

It was evening and too dark to distinguish faces when he was in the street.

I wouldn't recognize him even if I knew which way he had gone, the man thought, hurrying along the dark streets, looking at the strange people he passed in the dark, who passed without looking at him. Once a bus went roaring by with a smell of burnt oil and he felt the sickness coming at him again but he fought it back and walked faster and it was all right and he was only a hollow man walking in the darkness without objective. Once a stranger asked him where he was going, but he went on without stopping to think that he did not know the answer. And once somewhere far off in the dark something hurt for a second because of the girl left alone and crying: but that was over immediately.

Then he was out of the town and the moon was up but behind cloud and it was less dark, and then he was walking on grass and he could see the heavy black swelling shapes of the downs, and the clouds sculptured in towers and bastions and battlemented with the light of the climbing moon. Then there was first the smell and then the sound of the sea. Then there were cliffs and the cold tumultuous restless water beneath.

Then instead of hurrying he was standing still, he was very tired now and sweating under the heavy coat, and looking up he saw a white shining fan, spreading over the sky, like light from a door slowly opening, and he knew the moon was coming out of the clouds. Then he looked over the sea and there were islands it seemed, and then a great migration of birds thickened the air and he was in a rushing of wings, the wings beat so dark and fast round him he felt dizzy like falling and the moon disappeared. And then it was clear again, brilliant moonlight, and there, ahead, bright as day, were all the small islands, Cape Promise, and the bay of Mairangi, wide, still, unbelievably peaceful under the full moon. And then he did know where he was going.

'I CAN'T remember anything that happened,' the boy said. 'It was like a blackout, sort of.'

He twisted his thin body uneasily on the couch where he was lying, and for a second his face, which seemed much too startled and meek and vulnerable for a soldier's face, was turned up towards the doctor sitting beside him; then he looked very quickly away.

Queer sort of looking bloke for a doctor, he thought, noticing transiently beside his shoulders the crossed legs in shabby grey trousers, the worn brogues with mended soles. He wished that the doctor were not there. The doctor's presence made him uneasy, although there was nothing to cause uneasiness about the look of the man.

The couch was comfortable. If he had been alone in the room the boy would have quite enjoyed lying there with a pillow under his head. The room was small and there was nothing at all alarming about it. The walls were pale green, enclosing no furniture but the couch, the chair on which the doctor sat, and a desk. There was a calendar with a bright picture hanging over the desk. The boy could not see what was in the picture because, in order to look at it properly, he would have had to turn his head round in the doctor's direction. The sun was shining outside the window which was open a bit at the top. The glass panes had been broken in a raid and replaced by an opaque plastic substance so that you couldn't see out. The boy wondered what was outside the window. He thought he would like, vaguely, to get up, open the bottom half of the window, and have a look: and also to examine the picture on the calendar. The presence of the doctor prohibited him from doing these things, so he looked down at his hospital tie and began fidgeting with the loose ends of it. The tie had been washed so often that it had faded from red to deep pink and the cotton fabric had a curious dusty pile on it, almost like velvet, which communicated an agreeable sensation to the tips of his fingers.

32

'Which is the last day you can remember clearly?' the doctor asked.

'The day I was due to rejoin my unit,' the boy said, reluctantly detaching a fragment of his attention from the pleasant feel of the tie.

'Do you remember what date it was?'

'September the eleventh.' He wasn't likely to forget that date, so hypnotically, fascinated with dread, he had watched it racing towards him through the telescoped days of his embarkation leave.

'Do you know what the date is to-day?'

He shook his head, looking down at the tie, and his very fine, limp hair fluffed on the pillow where it was longest on the top of his head.

'It's the eighteenth. You started remembering things when you were brought in here yesterday: so that means your blackout lasted five complete days, doesn't it?'

'Yes, I suppose so,' the boy said; and waited, in apprehension, for the bad part to begin.

Why can't they leave you alone? he was thinking. Why must they go on poking and prodding at you when all you wanted was to be left in peace? It wasn't as if you would ever be able to tell them what they wanted to know, or as if they'd ever understand if you did. His fingers, pleating the ends of the tie, gripped more abruptly the softness from which they no longer derived any satisfaction.

'You remember everything that happened while you were on leave quite distinctly?' the doctor asked him.

'Yes, oh yes,' the boy said at once, speaking fast, as if he hoped, by bringing the words out quickly, in some way to terminate the matter without touching on what was most painful.

'And where did you spend this leave?'

There now, it's begun now, the bad part's beginning, he thought in himself. And recognizing helplessly the preliminary movement of that thing which from the outset had filled him with a profound unease he remained silent now, while his mind ran from side to side, seeking the unknown avenues of defence or escape.

'Well, where did you spend your leave?'

The doctor's voice was casual and almost friendly, but there was much firmness in it, and also there came along with it the dangerous thing preparing to launch its attack, which could not be trifled with.

'I went home to my auntie,' the boy said, whispering.

Like looking back down a long tunnel he began remembering now that tenement place off the Wandsworth Road, the water-tap out on the landing and the room always chockablock with the washing and cooking and the dirty dishes and pots that his mum never could keep upsides with, what with her heart, and his dad coming in drunk as often as not and knocking her about till the neighbours started opening their doors and threatening to call a policeman: and himself feeling shaky and sick and trying not to make a noise with his crying as he hid there crouched up in a ball of misery under the table. His auntie used to come visiting sometimes when his dad was away, and she was not old at all, or frightening or frightened at all, but so pretty and young and gay, that maybe that was the reason he always thought the word auntie was a word you used as a kind of endearment, in the way sweetie and honey were used. When he was eight years old his dad got t.b. and gave up the drink, but it was too late then, his mum was dying already, and when his dad died later on in the san he felt only happier than he had ever been in his life because he was going to live with his auntie for ever and ever and there would be no more shouts or rows or crying or staring neighbours.

He remembered the little dark house where the two of them lived then in Bracken's Court; tiny and old-fashioned and a bit inconvenient it was with those steep stairs with a kink in them where his dad would surely have broken his neck if he'd ever come there after closing time: but cosy too, like a dolls' house, and they'd always been happy in it together, even after the arthritis stopped his auntie from going out to her dressmaking. When he left school he'd been taken on as messenger at the stationer's, and later had got a salesman's job inside the shop and worked hard and was getting along well, so that it hadn't seemed to matter too much that she could do less and less of the work they sent her at home, because he was earning almost enough to take care of them both and soon it would be more than enough the way things were going. Then the war had come, and she had got worse, she had those bad headaches often and couldn't manage the crooked stairs. Then he had been called up and he had hated it all, hated the army, hated leaving home, hated losing his good job, hated the idea of being sent overseas to fight: but most of all hated leaving her badly off now, financially insecure, bombs falling perhaps, and she alone with her crippling pains and no one reliable to take care of her; she who had always been sweet and lovely to him, and deserved taking care of more than anyone in the world. When he thought of what might become of her if he were taken prisoner or killed it was more than he could bear and he almost wished she were safely out of it all. Yes, when she went down with 'flu or whatever it was during his last leave, he almost hoped she wouldn't get well, it broke his heart so to leave her like that. But these were some of the things which never could be explained and he only wished to be left alone and not be made to remember.

But the questions had to go on.

'What are the last things you remember doing before you left your aunt's house that final day?' the doctor wanted to know.

'I spent a goodish time straightening up and cleaning the place so as to leave everything shipshape,' the boy said. 'My auntie being an invalid more or less I wanted to leave things as easy for her as I could.'

Out of the end of his left eye he could see the doctor's crossed knees and the feet in their mended shoes, and for an instant rebellion rose in him because this was a man no different from himself who by no divine right of class or wealth or any accepted magic sought to force memory on him. But there was something beyond that: beyond just the man who could be opposed with obstinacy there was the frightening thing which he had to fight in the dark, and he knew that he dared not remain silent because his silence might be to that thing's advantage, and he went on, speaking low and mumbling as if the words came out against their will.

'We had tea about four. Then I went up and packed my kit. Then it was time to go for the train. I said good-bye and started for the station. King's Cross I had to go from.'

There was a long pause, and at the end of it came the doctor's voice asking if that was the last thing he could remember, and the boy's voice telling him that it was, and then there was silence again.

'That's queer,' the boy said suddenly into this silence. And now his voice sounded changed, there was astonishment and dismay in it, and the doctor uncrossed his knees and looked at him more closely, asking him, 'What's queer?'

'I've just remembered something,' the boy said. 'That time I told you about when I left the house, it wasn't the last time, really.'

'Not the last time you were in the house?'

'No. I've just remembered. It's just sort of come back to me somehow. When I'd gone part of the way to the station I found I'd left something important behind, my pay-book I think it was, and I had to sprint back to fetch it.'

The doctor took a packet of cigarettes out of his pocket and lighted one with his utility lighter which never worked the first time he thumbed it, and blew out a little smoke. He seemed in no hurry at all about asking the next question.

'Can you remember how you were feeling when you went back?'

'I suppose I felt a bit flustered like anyone would about leaving my pay-book,' the boy said, defensive suddenly, and blindly suspicious of some unimagined trap.

Looking into the tunnel he remembered fumbling under the mat for the key which was left there for the next-door woman who came in to give a hand. Was it as he came in or as he was going out again that he stood at the foot of the stairs where they crooked in the angle of a dog's hindleg out of the living-room? It was dusk, and he remembered the silence inside the house as though there were a dead person or somebody sleeping upstairs. Yes, she must have been asleep then, he thought: but whether he went up to her was not in the memory, but only the noise of his army boots clattering away on the paving-stones of the court, and as he came out into the high street a church bell was ringing.

The doctor asked, 'What happened afterwards?'

'I can't remember anything more,' the boy said.

'Nothing whatever? Not even some isolated detail?'

'Yes,' he said, after a while. 'I think I remember looking for the station entrance, and a big bridge with a train shunting on it up high.'

He was aware, just then, of danger skirmishing all about in the green-walled room, and lying there on the couch his eyes were still down where they seemed safe on the pink ends of the tie, his hands clenched now and his neck and shoulders gone tense; and he not knowing if it were through his words or his silence that the danger would strike.

Why did a church bell keep ringing in the tunnel like that? It was a very deep tunnel into which he was being forced. He did not want to go down in the tunnel again. He was afraid. But because of the unknown thing whose immediate agent was the casual, near-friendly voice nothing could save him from that black exploration split by the doleful and ugly clang of a distant bell.

'As if someone had died,' he said out loud.

'Who do you think might have died?'

No, no. Not that. Don't let it come, the boy thought, fighting desperately against what had all the time been waiting there behind every word; the worst thing, the intolerable pain, the fear not to be borne. And at once his nerves started to twitch and tears sprang in his eyes in case she might not have been sleeping but dead in the silent room at the top of the steep stairs, investigated or not by him he was, agonizingly, somehow unable to know.

Running in panic along the tunnel he remembered the alley-way, like something in a film he'd seen once, blank walls leaning nearer and nearer to suffocation, and, at the bend, a lamp-bracket sticking out with a dangling noose; only no corpse was at the end of the rope. And always the hurrying army boots and the bell ringing, till he did not know if it was the noise of his own steps or the church bell clanging inside his head. The noise was part of his hunger, and he remembered, further along the tunnel, scrounging about at night where a street market had been and finding, finally, in the gutter, a piece of sausage, grey, slimy, like the wrist of a dead baby, and the terrible thirst that came on him afterwards, and how he drank out of a horse-trough, scooping the water up with his hands, and it seemed all wrong because they killed animals painlessly. Then there

37

was that open space, a heath or a common, where he had vomited and lain on the ground, his hair in the rough grass. He felt weak and stiff from the vomiting and clouds of insects were round him, settling on his face and hands and crawling over his mouth because he was too weak to flap at them, but in the end it got dark and the insects went away then and left him in peace.

Faster and faster he ran to escape from the tunnel and the tolling noise of the bell. And at last he was outside, the tunnel was getting smaller and smaller until it vanished, and there was respite from the tolling, nothing left now but the room with the doctor quietly smoking, sunshine outside the window, the calendar on the wall.

The boy was not lying on the couch any more but bending over with hunched shoulders as if hiding from something, his head on his raised knees in the posture a person might take crouching under a table: and though he was crying he was no longer thinking of the tunnel or of the dangerous secret thing which had scared him so terribly, or about anything he could have put into any words.

'It was like a blackout. A blackout. I can't remember,' he kept on hopelessly mumbling, amongst the tears.

GLORIOUS BOYS

WHY do I do this? she thought, walking with Mia in the cold London dark vibrant with the resonance of out-going bombers. Why do I ever go to a party, not knowing what to say or what to do with myself? Hands were easy with glasses and cigarettes, but the rest of the body, embarrassingly material, intractable, and absolutely unwilling to dissolve itself into a dew; how did one cope with it? How did one recognize the correct moment for putting it into a chair, opening its mouth and emitting appropriate sounds, propping it against the end of a sofa, getting it up and moving it across the room to confront some stranger's alarmingly expectant, or self-assured, and in every case utterly inaccessible countenance?

The terrifying independence of the body. Its endless opposition. The appalling underground movements of the nerves, muscles, viscera, upon which, like a hated and sadistic gauleiter, one unremittingly imposed an implacable repressive regime, threatened eternally by the equally implacable threat of insubordination. The perpetual fear of being sabotaged into some sudden shameful exposure.

Ahead the house waited uncompromising, the imminent dark objective. Why did I come here?

It was Mia, naturally, who had brought her. Mia, like a little infanta, like a little fantastic princess, not quite human exactly, daughter, not of a golden shower, but of a black-pearl passion, smoky dark hair and cheeks the lustrous blurred pink of the inside of those very elaborate shells, bright dress and improbable buckled shoes. Mia shooting her arrowy kindness not of earth or humanity into the heart: no warmth but only darting gleams from the progeny of a pearl. Why was I persuaded?

Can't say no, she was thinking while Mia opened the door and the noise, the special noise, smell, atmosphere, of a party came down to them from the top of the short white staircase leading directly into the large light smoky room. Can't say no; non-

39

specific depressive trait. The tedium of these everlasting psychological pigeonholes. And it wasn't true in her case either; at least, not entirely true. It wasn't only slackness, weak moral fibre, whatever you liked to call it. There was that other thing too, the force always driving one to open every door, cross every bridge, walk up every gangway.

They added their coats to the winter coats already piled and slipping from hidden pieces of furniture at the foot of the stairs. Now I would like to stop here for a little, the back of her mind reflected. Now I would like to spend a little time with the coats, knowing them, knowing their different characters, textures, smells, getting the feel through my fingers of the essential essence of coat, getting to know how it feels to be fur or tweed. But it won't do. Or rather, it isn't done. It simply is not done in normal society to waste time feeling oneself into a pile of coats. Odd how normal people have no time except for other people. Unless you're alone it's practically impossible ever to get to know the non-human things: it simply isn't allowed. There's something queer about you, people said if you tried to explain.

'Let's go in now,' the little clear voice of Mia said, rather high, like some blithe warm-country-frequenting bird; the jewelled kinglet, perhaps?

'I'm ready,' she said.

The preliminary staircase was much too short. Through introductions she was still back there on the stairs watching Mia's newly-combed hair floating so fine and like a darker smoke on the cigarette smoke thickened air. The dark downward smoke drifted past backs and bosoms; with confident and infrangible sprightliness the buckled shoes twinkled into the crowd.

The party, she said to herself, following on reluctant. I must be in the party. No more dreaming now. She had always dreamed too much in her life, dreamed when she ought to have been attending to people, and so lost all the prizes and antagonized everyone.

She thought how she had antagonized Frank by dreaming herself into this that seemed a crazy journey to him, to this country, away from safety and warmth, all across the world. She thought about being alone in the raid on the night she arrived, the night the post office was hit. She had stood watching out in the street, and while the big building burned, and she was feeling the anguish of exploded walls, burst roof, torn girders wrenching away, smoke, flames, blinding up, spouting up through the crazy avalanching of stone, the crashing, ruinous death of all that mass of stone and durability struck down with a single blow, a warden had shouted to her from the post not to stand woolgathering but to get under cover away from the shell splinters that were coming down. There had been rage in his voice to blast her out of the dream. But the warden's anger and Frank's anger couldn't be helped and were irrelevant really, since she knew she could never cure herself of the woolgathering.

The man talking to her now had a red face and his hair was curly, sandy and grey mixed, like wool.

If only he doesn't start asking questions, she thought. If only he doesn't know or care that I've only been over here a few months. If only I don't have to try and say something convincing. As she was merely doing her own work and was not on a war assignment, people wondered why she had come all that difficult voyage from the safe underside of the world. For the questions which followed then she had no adequate answers. All her life the force had been operative in her, the insistent unknown thing that drove her to open the doors, to walk up the gangways, to leave security when it became familiar, in no spirit of gallant adventure, but terrified; though the terror, certainly, was inside the dream where also the inexorable voice commanded, Move on there, traveller; other places, experiences, wait for investigation. It was obvious that no explanation was possible.

Someone gave her a glass with punch in it, hot and faintly steaming, and she felt the comfortable warmth of the glass in her hand and lifted the glass and smelled the sweet, warm, raffish smell of the rum which had a curl of apple peel floating in it. There were lighted candles about the room and silver stars because it was Christmas time.

'They've got some interesting pictures here,' she said. And because it was all right and allowed to be interested in pictures and to get to know them she moved over to stand in front of the canvas, pale bird's egg sea, sand, and a pink house — it looked like a Christopher Wood, and the woolly man moved too and looked for a moment and murmured and moved away, set free to talk to some more congenial guest.

What exactly is it that's wrong with me? What is the thing about me that people never can take? her thoughts wandered, although she knew the answer perfectly well. It was the woolgathering, of course, the preoccupation with non-human things, the interest in the wrong place, that was so unacceptable. People took it as an insult. Intuitively they resented it even if they were unaware of it. And fundamentally they were right; it was insulting from their point of view. But why did she care what they felt? There was nothing to be done anyway. The woolgathering was far stronger than she was.

She stood and looked at the picture a little; gradually, as she saw no one noticing her, allowing her eyes to stray to less approved objects, the candelabra, the stars, the pagodas on the long yellow curtains. A carnation pinned to a dress with the coloured badge of a regiment came between, and behind this the known and utterly unlikely face from another country suddenly sprang out at her in the room like a pistol pointed over the noise and smoke and the atmosphere of a party and for a second she felt cold and confused with the countries running wildly together.

Then he came forward, blocking out the carnation and standing in front in the blue flying uniform that was different only in the word on the shoulder from the uniform an English pilot would wear. He had a very young face and bright bloodshot eyes that did not look quite natural. His face still looks so young, she thought; but his body was different. Over there his body had been self-conscious in uniform and had looked inappropriate in that dress, but now the uniform was part of him and did not look strange on him in any way. He and she and Frank had laughed together about the uniform over there, calling him the blue orchid, but now there was nothing to laugh at at all and she wondered how it could ever have seemed funny that he should be wearing it.

'I don't believe it. I just don't believe it's you,' he was saying.

'Hello,' she said. 'What an incredible meeting. What are you doing here?'

'Week-end leave.'

'Do you know these people, then?'

'A friend brought me. I thought I'd like some social life for a change.'

'I'm very glad to see you, Ken.'

'I'd have got in touch with you if I'd known your address. Now I've got to go back to-morrow. Too queer running into you this way.'

'It's extraordinary. Absolutely extraordinary.' While they were speaking she saw on his face small new lines of eye-strain but otherwise nothing altered. But the eyes themselves looked like the eyes of a man waiting to ride a difficult race. There was the same fixity and the brightness did not seem natural.

'Do you remember the last time we saw each other?' she asked him.

'The morepork,' he said, smiling.

She did not smile. She was very startled, somehow, that he should remember and more startled that the picture should come up so clearly then. Sometimes the picture was there at night and sometimes it came when she was alone and she could understand that; but now in the noise of the party it came so much stronger and clearer than it should and there was the low house at the end of the point with water on three sides and there were the big trees with cormorants in them, and she had been happier there with Frank than with other men she had been around with but she had left it as she left every place; and there it was clear in the picture, only it startled her now. That picture was part of the woolgathering and most nights she saw it. It was very familiar but it startled her still, especially coming clear in the crowded room with the lights and the party voices, the room inside it wasn't like this room. It was plainer and emptier, no stars or candles although there were glasses, only the three people there, the troopship waiting for Ken down in the harbour, she herself waiting to travel towards the war in another

43

ship, the morepork calling outside, the ill-omened bird of disaster. Frank laughing about the native superstition, holding his hands tight on the arms of the chair to keep from getting up and shouting to scare the bastard away. Knowing all the good well-known things that were ending. Knowing the danger and the loss and all the rest that mustn't be spoken. Knowing exactly what bad-luck symbols were worth. One could scare the morepork away but that would make everything worse. And there was Frank, gruesomely enough, joking badly about it, for whom the morepork calls; and perhaps it was calling out for all three of us really, we used to watch between the trees on the point when the ships lined up for the convoys and she could see those trees every time in the picture with the cormorants, wings held out stiff to dry, like small scarecrows. But that was another country and why was it here now? When it came at night or when she was by herself that was all right. But coming sudden and inopportune it confused her as now, she standing glass in hand at a party, talking to Ken with his unnatural eyes and he looking entirely too natural in the damned uniform. She lifted her glass and drank out of it; the punch had gone cold. Ken was still smiling. She lowered the glass again.

The woolgathering was part of her and she was not troubled by it except when it came between her and the people she wanted; and the fear that she would finally lose the last chance. That was all that was troubling in that. Being queer didn't matter much. She didn't worry about being different and queer but what startled her so that she felt cold in the warm room was the low brown house appearing and the morepork calling outside. The picture could not really be at the party, she had heard the morepork call, and there was no morepork. Nor was there any sense in believing in evil omens. Then what was she hearing and looking at and what was disturbing, and why did she feel colder than she had felt in the cold streets because of a picture and a bird's mournful cry thousands of miles away underneath the world?

She put her glass down on a little table amongst cactuses. It must be obvious, she was thinking. It must be obvious to everyone that she felt the way she was feeling. Ken surely would notice something.

It was suddenly imperative that she escape from the eyes that were surely collecting. This was the sort of thing you got let in for by being the way she was. This was the work of the saboteur in the nerves.

'I must go, Ken,' she said, hoping it didn't sound stupidly urgent.

He did not express surprise. He said, 'I wanted to talk to you.'

'Come back to my place, then. It's not far and we'll have something to eat there. One can't talk at a party, anyway.'

The words came without thought, and then, seeing the hesitation or whatever it was on his face, she remembered to think and said, 'Oh, but of course you don't want to come away from the party. Good-bye.'

But he was behind her when she said something to the host and to Mia and when she went downstairs and pulled her coat from the pile he was still there and held it up for her while she put it on. Only when the closed door shut out the noise of the party and the sinister noise of the bombers was back again deep and strong and inevitable as if it would always be filling the sky day and night, as if it were the noise of the earth's self revolving, he hesitated and seemed to hold on to the handle of the closed door so that she wondered if he would really rather have stayed. But he came with her into the street.

'Shall we go by bus or by tube?' she asked him. With distant surprise she heard him answer at once, 'By tube', when he couldn't have known which was better, not knowing where she lived.

The moon was up now showing the empty bed of the street and the black bank of the opposite houses and the whitened, moon-frosted roofs which might have been snowy escarpments. It was all very drear and deserted and becoming traditional and no different from the other cities unlighted and waiting amongst their ruins under the moon. In her travelling she had seen so many cities change over from darkness to light, and she remembered suddenly and completely a harbour at nightfall, the waterfront brilliant with lights, the lost sun still ghostly gold on the Kaikoura mountains across the Strait.

'It's queer how it grows on you,' he said. They were walking towards the tube station.

'What?'

'Having one's life up there instead of on the ground.' She saw his face lifted up to the noise of the planes and his head tilted. 'I don't feel at home down here. I don't belong any more. There seems to be no place where I fit in. I wanted to feel like other people again, so I thought I'd go to parties and talk to women and that would make it all right. But it doesn't work out somehow. I still feel outside. I'd like to be the same as I used to be and feel like other people again.'

'I suppose you never write anything now?'

'Good God, no.'

What a fiendishly efficient machine war is, she thought, remembering him as he was and the writing, a bit immature but sensitive and direct and with much integrity. Now he would never write the things he might have written when he had learned to write well enough. It destroyed very thoroughly this war machine, this incinerator of individuality and talent and life, forging the sensitive and creative young into the steel fabric of death, turning them out by the million, the murder men, members of Murder Inc., the big firm, the global organization. Suddenly, she felt acutely angry with him.

'How could you let them do it to you?' she said. 'How can you let us all down?'

He was not listening, walking beside her in the uniform that he wore as if he had never worn anything else. He was walking too fast for her, like a man in a hurry to get somewhere, and now he said, looking up still at the throbbing sky, 'They've got a great night for it,' and she said, 'The others have too.'

'I'd hate to be on the ground in a bad raid,' he said. 'I certainly would hate to be down here.' He stared up at the sky.

'Don't you ever think what it is you're doing up there?' she asked him.

They were at the tube station, and going into the light she noticed again in his eyes the nervous intent look of a rider waiting for the start of a hard race, his movements rather jerky and stiff, and she

46

began to feel sorry because something was wrong somewhere. She looked to see what was wrong, but in place of the man with the young face who looked at her with bright bloodshot eyes there came the house in another country and the trees with cormorants in them and the morepork was calling and there was no way of seeing anything else.

Then in the train it was gone and she attended to him again: but now with anger reviving in her he was only the murder man, and having no clear idea of the inside of a plane, she saw only an anonymous robot, padded, helmeted, hung about with accoutrements and surrounded by switches and dials, sowing catastrophe from a lighted box in the sky.

'How do you ever sleep?' she asked the man who was sitting by her in the blue clothes, here, in the underground. 'Don't you feel frightened to go to sleep?'

'It's our people or theirs. You know that.'

'I know that because there's a murder committed next door all the rest of us in the street don't have to start killing our neighbours.'

'It's war,' he said. 'I simply do my job. Do you suppose I enjoy bombing civilians? Is it my fault?'

'Yes,' she said. 'If you know what you're doing and acquiesce in it that makes you guilty.'

'No. You're not fair.'

She looked at him and saw his eyes screwed up painfully as they would be when he looked into the sun. The wrinkles around his eyes looked strange on the young face, almost like painted lines.

'Listen,' she said. 'The morepork was calling for you all right. This is the worst badness that could have happened to you, that you should turn into a murderer.'

The train was stopped in a station and a woman, hearing, turned in the doorway as she was getting out and said, 'How dare you speak like that to one of our glorious boys?' Then the doors slid shut in front of her outraged face and Ken made a sound like a laugh that was not really amused and she, sitting beside him, laughed too and said, 'Spreading dismay and despondency among His Majesty's forces. I could be put in jail.'

47

And, because of the laughter, she recognized the young face for which, somewhere, she had had some affection, regretting again dimly the eyes strained and screwed up as if they were hurting, and said, 'Don't take any notice of me; I suppose I'm a bit crazy', falling easily into the pattern she ran her life by.

That was the easy pattern, to let people think she was a little mad. And it was true that she was a way they never would be able to understand, with the woolgathering, and now the picture and that bad luck bird that had come with Ken in the light in front of them all. She heard him say, 'It's all right', and then there was nothing more said and it was time to get out of the train.

The platform was crowded and most of the bunks occupied. Here and there people slept already and a man near the tea urns was wandering up and down selling buns from a tray slung on a strap round his neck. There were more shelterers than there usually were.

'Warning's just gone,' one of them said, close to her, as they passed, and Ken said quickly, 'What?'

'The warning,' she told him, stopping because he had stood still suddenly. 'The glorious boys in the different uniform.'

Of course it's lunacy: we've all of us gone insane, she said to herself, thinking of the planes streaming out, crossing the incoming enemy stream up there in the freezing sky. Did they signal like passing ships or just ignore one another? The demented human race destroying itself with no god or external sanity intervening. Well, let them get on with it. Let it be over soon. She was very tired of the war-world and only wanted everything to be over. It seemed not to matter any more what happened. There had been far too much happen already. Queer how tired apprehending a war made you. The war had always been there in the different countries, but it had taken London to bring her the apprehension of war. This can't go on, she thought sometimes, waking suddenly in the night or moving about a room: this can *not* go on. But it went on and on and she went on somehow, only feeling always more and more tired. She thought a little about how tired she was.

Walking along the platform, keeping pace with Ken who walked slowly now, the woolgathering took possession of her and all the way up in the lift she was dreaming the double stream of destruction, feeling the composite entity of the bomber-streams, gigantic cruising serpents of metal horror circling and smashing the world.

Guns were firing and searchlights were setting their geometrical snares when they came out of the station. The searchlights had not caught anything. They closed and opened and closed and drew blank again.

'Hadn't we better wait a bit?' Ken said.

'It's only a minute from here and there doesn't seem to be any shrapnel,' she answered, not quite out of the woolgathering.

She started along the pavement in black shadow. There would be moonlight on that side of the street when they turned the corner. The moon was just past the full. It was under this moon that, walking home by herself, she had seen the morepork perched on the roof and calling its ominous cry. The budgerigars in their cage twittered with fright. No, that was somewhere else. Where was that? Her eyes refusing the lighted sky she was not sure what part of her life she was in; and then she was back from wherever it was to the war and the war-locked town.

The gunfire died down briefly and a plane began making its familiar maddening, hysterical, unescapable sound. She did not notice at first that Ken had stopped walking beside her. Then the noise of the plane got louder and she remembered about him and he was not there and that startled her and the night seemed unreal. Looking back then, she could see a darker bulk against the dark wall of a house, and she got the torch out of her bag and flashed it and saw his face lifted and turned to the sky. The light fell full on his face and she looked once and switched off the torch quickly and went to him and said, 'Ken'. But the guns started again and he did not look at her but moved away fast, looking up, back towards the tube station, the way they had just come.

She called, 'Ken, Ken'. And then, not knowing where the words came from or thinking them even, 'Oh, no, no. Oh, please no. Oh, Ken'.

There was no answer, it was hard to hear anything in the barrage, but she heard footsteps running.

In the sky, the laborious searchlights exultantly caught and clamped a desperate plunging speck in their trap. But she did not see it because quite suddenly her eyes were too full of tears.

BEFORE they took over the big house and turned it into a psychiatric hospital the room must have been somebody's boudoir. It was upstairs, quite a small room, with a painted ceiling of cupids and flowers and doves, the walls divided by plaster mouldings to simulate pillars and wreaths, and the panels between the mouldings sky blue. It was a frivolous little room. The name Dr. Pope looked like a mistake on the door and so did the furniture which was not at all frivolous but ugly and utilitarian, the big office desk, the rather ominous high, hard thing that was neither a bed nor a couch.

Dr. Pope did not look at all frivolous either. He was about forty, tall, straight, muscular, with a large, impersonal, hairless, tidy face, rather alarmingly alert and determined looking. He did not look in the least like a holy father, or, for that matter, like any sort of a father. If one thought of him in terms of the family he was more like an efficient and intolerant elder brother who would have no patience with the weaknesses of younger siblings.

Dr. Pope came into his room after lunch, walking fast as he always did, and shut the door after him. He did not look at the painted ceiling or out of the open window through which came sunshine and the pleasant rustle of trees. Although the day was warm he wore a thick dark double-breasted suit and did not seem hot in it. He sat down at once at the desk.

There was a pile of coloured folders in front of him. He took the top folder from the pile and opened it and began reading the typed case notes inside. He read carefully, with the easy concentration of an untroubled singlemindedness. Occasionally, if any point required consideration, he looked up from the page and stared reflectively at the blue wall over the desk where he had fastened with drawing pins a number of tables and charts. These pauses for reflection never lasted more than a few seconds; he made his decisions quickly and they were final. He went on steadily reading, holding his fountain pen and sometimes making a note on the typescript in firm, small, legible handwriting.

Presently there was a knock and he called out, 'Come in'.

'Will you sign this pass, please, for Sergeant Hunter?' a nurse said, coming up to the desk.

She put a yellow slip on the desk and the doctor said, 'Oh, yes', and signed it impatiently and she picked it up and put a little sheaf of hand-written pages in its place and he, starting to read through these new papers with the impatience gone from his manner, said, 'Ah, the ward reports', in a different voice that sounded interested and eager.

The nurse stood looking over his shoulder at the writing, most of which was her own.

'Excellent. Excellent,' Dr. Pope said after a while. He glanced up at the waiting nurse and smiled at her. She was his best nurse, he had trained her himself in his own methods, and the result was entirely satisfactory. She was an invaluable and trustworthy assistant who understood what he was trying to do, approved of his technique, and co-operated intelligently. 'Really excellent work', he repeated, smiling.

She smiled back and for a moment the identical look of gratification on the two faces gave them a curious resemblance to one another, almost as if they were near relatives, although they were not really alike at all.

'Yes,' she said, 'we're certainly getting results now. The general morale in the wards has improved enormously.' Then her face became serious again and she said, 'If only we could get Ward Six into line'.

The smile simultaneously disappeared from the doctor's face and a look that was more characteristic appeared there; a look of impatience and irritation. He turned the pages in front of him and re-read one of them and the irritated expression became fixed.

'Yes, I see. Ward Six again. I suppose it's that fellow Williams making a nuisance of himself as usual?'

'It's impossible to do anything with him.' The nurse's cool voice contained annoyance behind its coolness. 'He's a bad type, I'm afraid. Obstructive and stubborn. Unfortunately some of the youngsters and the less stable men are apt to be influenced by his talk. He's always stirring up discontent in the ward.'

'These confounded trouble-makers are a menace to our whole work,' Dr. Pope said. 'Rebellious undesirables. I think friend Williams will have to be got rid of.' He pulled a scribbling pad across the desk and wrote the name Williams on it, pressing more heavily on the pen than he usually did so that the strokes of the letters came very black. He underlined the name with deliberation and drew a circle round it and pushed the pad back to its place and asked in a brisker tone:

'Anyone else in Six giving trouble?'

'I've been rather worried about Kling the last day or two.'

'Kling? What's he been up to?'

'He seems very depressed, doctor.'

'You think his condition's deteriorating?'

'Well, he seems to be getting more depersonalized and generally inaccessible. There's no knowing what's in his head. It's not the language difficulty either; his English is perfectly good. But he's hardly spoken a word since that day he was put in the gardening squad and got so upset.'

'Oh, yes; the gardening incident. Odd, getting such a violent reaction there. It should give one a lead if there were time to go into it. But there isn't, of course. That's the worst of dealing with large numbers of patients as we are.' A shade of regret on the doctor's face faded out as he said to the nurse still standing beside him:

'You see far more of Kling than I do. What's your own opinion of him?'

'I think, personally, that he's got something on his mind. Something he won't talk about.'

'Make him talk, then. That's your job.'

'I've tried, of course. But it's no good. Perhaps he's afraid to talk. He's shut himself up like an oyster.'

'Oysters can be opened,' the doctor said. He twisted his chair round and smiled directly up at the good nurse he had trained. He was very pleased with her and with himself. In spite of troublesome individuals like Williams and Kling the work of the hospital was going extremely well. 'Provided, naturally, that one has the right implement with which to open them.'

He got up and stood with his back to the window which to be in keeping with the room's decoration should have had satin curtains but instead was framed in dusty blackout material. He had his hands in his trouser pockets and he was still smiling as he went on, 'We might try a little forcible opening on oyster Kling'.

The nurse nodded and made a sound of agreement and prepared to go, holding the signed pass in her hand.

'Lovely day, isn't it?' she remarked on her way, in order not to end the interview too abruptly.

Dr. Pope glanced into the sunshine and turned his back on it again.

'I'll be glad when the summer's over,' he said. 'Everyone's efficiency level drops in this sort of weather. Give me the cold days when we're all really keen and on our toes.'

The nurse went out and shut the door quietly.

The doctor swung round again in his energetic fashion and opened the window as wide as it would go, looking out over grassy grounds dark with evergreens. On a hard tennis court to the right a circle of patients in shorts clumsily and apathetically threw a football about and he watched them just long enough to observe the bored slackness of their instructor's stance and to note automatically that the man was due for a reprimand. Then he went back to his desk under the smiling loves.

As if he were somehow aware of the doctor's censorious eye, the instructor outside just then straightened up and shouted with perfunctory disgust, 'You there, Kling, or whatever your name is; wake up, for Christ's sake, can't you?'

The man who had not been ready when the ball was thrown to him, who had, in fact, altogether forgotten why he was supposed to be standing there on the hot reddish plane marked with arbitrary white lines, looked first at the instructor before bending down to the ball which had bounced off his leg and was slowly spinning on the gritty surface in front of him. He picked up the big ball and held it in both hands as though he did not know what to do with it, as though he could conceive of no possible connection between himself and this hard spherical object. Then, after a moment, he tossed it towards the man standing next to him in the ring, not more than two yards away, and at once forgot it again and nothing remained of the incident in his mind except the uneasy resentment that always came now when anyone called out to him.

For many months he had been called Kling, that being the first syllable and not the whole of his name which was too difficult for these tongues trained in a different pronunciation. To start with he had not minded the abbreviation, had even felt pleased because, like a nickname, it seemed to admit him to comradeship with the others. But now, for a long time, he had resented it. They've taken everything from me, even my name, he thought sometimes when the sullen misery settled on him. By 'they' he did not mean the men of another race with whom he shared sleeping room and food and daily routine, or any particular individuals, but just the impersonal machine that had caught and mauled him and dragged him away from the two small lakes and the mountains where his home was, far off to this flat country across the sea.

And then there was that other reason why the sound of the short syllable was disturbing.

The game, if it could be called that, came to an end and the patients slowly dispersed. There was a little free time left before tea. Some of the men walked back to the hospital, others lighted cigarettes and stood talking in groups, several lay full length on the grass or dawdled where evergreens spread heavy mats of shade.

Kling sat down by himself on the top of a little bank. He was young, very big and broad, very well built if you didn't mind that depth of chest, dark, his hair wiry like a black dog's, arms muscled for labour, his eyes only slightly decentred. He did not look ill at all, he looked enormously strong, only his movements were all rather stiff and slow, there was a marked unnatural rigidity about the upper part of his torso because of the lately healed wound and because of that heavy thing he carried inside him.

The bank was in full sunshine. Kling sat there sweating, dark stains spreading on his singlet under the arms, sharp grasses pricking his powerful, bare, hairy legs, his breast stony feeling, waiting for time to pass. He was not consciously waiting. His apathy was so profound that it was not far removed from unconsciousness. A breeze blew and the tall grass rippled gently but he did not know. He did not know that the sun shone. His head was bent and the only movements about him were his slow breaths and the slowly widening stains on the singlet. His chest was hot and wet and gloom ached in the rocky weight the black stone weighed under his breastbone, and his big blackish eyes, dilated with gloom, stared straight ahead, only blinking when the sun dazzle hurt, and sweat stood in the deep horizontal lines on his forehead.

While he sat there a row of patients with gardening tools, spades, rakes, hoes, on their shoulders, came near. They walked in single file in charge of a man walking alongside, himself in hospital clothes, but with stripes on his sleeve. Kling watched them coming. All of him that still lived, resentment, gloom, misery, and all his clouded confusion, slowly tightened towards alarm. He could see the polished edges of spades shining and he shuddered, all his consciousness gathering into fear because of the danger signals coming towards him across the grass. As he watched his breathing quickened to heave his chest up and down, and, as the gardening squad reached the foot of the bank, he made a clumsy scramble and stood up.

Standing, he heard the clink of metal, and saw a shiny surface flash in the sun. The next moment he was running; stumbling stiffly, grappling the weight inside him, running from the men with the spades.

He heard the *Kling!* of his name being shouted, and again a second clattering *kling!* and running heard the spade kling-clink on the stone, he seemed to be holding it now, grasping the handle that slipped painfully in his wet hands, levering the blade under the huge ugly stone and straining finally as another frantic *kling!* came from the spade, and the toppling, heavy, leaden bulk of the stone fell and the old, mutilated face was hidden beneath, and Kling, stopping at the door of Ward Six where he had run, choking with strangled breath, while two men passing gazed at him in surprise, felt the dead mass of stone crushing his own breast.

He went into the ward and lay down on his bed and closed his eyes against the drops of sweat which trickled into the ends of his eyes. Then for a time there was nothing but the soreness of breath struggling against the stone.

This was what he had known a long while, ever since the truck had been blown thirty feet down into the ravine and he had seen the falling stone and felt it strike, felt it smash bone, tearing through muscle, sinew and vein to lodge itself immovably in his breast. Ever since then the stone had been there inside him, and at first it had seemed a small stone, just a dead spot, a sort of numbness under the breastbone. He had told the M.O. about it and the M.O. had laughed, saying there was no stone or possibility of a stone, and after that he had not spoken of it again; never once. But from the start he had been very uneasy, oppressed by the stone and by the heaviness that could come from it suddenly to drive away laughter and talk. He had tried not to think of the stone, but it had grown heavier and heavier until he could not think of anything else, until it crushed out everything else, and he could only carry it by making a very great effort. That was not so bad really, because with the weight of the stone crushing him he was nothing and that was not painful or frightening — it was just a waiting and that was nothing as well. But sometimes, perhaps at the moment of going to sleep, the dead weight lifted a little and then there were all the uncovered faces, the stone and the digging, and the old man would come back.

And so he lay very still on the bed, waiting for the deadness to overlay him, lying there in the knowledge that if the dead weight of the stone lifted to let him breathe the old man would come.

Strange how it was always this one who came and never one of the others.

The stone weight was lifting now and Kling, who had dozed a little while after his breath had stopped struggling, woke suddenly, frightened by the return of the bloody-faced man lying in brown leaves with hairs growing out of his nostrils and a torn shirt fluttering.

That was his father who had lain dead in the room beside the Blue Lake. No, not that man. When he thought of his home he couldn't see any faces, only the jagged line of the mountains like broken eggshell against the sky; and the two lakes, the Blue Lake and the lake shaped like a harp. That, and sometimes the inn with the acid wine of the district greenish in thick glasses, the swarming trout in the small tank on the wall, crowded sleek fish bodies slithering past the glass. But no faces ever. The stone blocked out all the home faces.

When he thought of the war it was always the digging he thought of because, seeing him so strong and used to work with a spade, they had put him on that job from the beginning; and then there were faces, wrecked or fearful or quiet or obscene faces, far too many of them, how he had laboured and toiled till his saliva ran sour, desperate to hide the faces away from the brutal light.

How many faces had he covered with earth and stones? There surely were thousands; and always thousands more waiting: and he all the time digging demented, always the compulsive urge in him like a frenzy, to hide the ruined faces away. And sometimes he remembered that officer in charge of the burying party, the one who joked and sang all the time; he must have been a bit cracked really, boozed or something, but they had dug and shovelled till their hands were raw blistered and hardly noticed the pain because of his Hey! Hi! Ho! and the jolly loud voice that he had.

There had been no singing that afternoon in the gully where the corpses, boys and old men among them, sprawled in the withered oak leaves between the rocks. Only haste then and the bitter taste in the mouth and the aching lungs, hacking the stony ground that was hard like iron to the weak bite of the spade, and the sky grey and muggy and flat and quiet. In the end someone had shouted and the others all started running back to the truck and he had run too and just then he had seen the old man lying flat on his back with blood congealing all down one side of his shattered face and the dry leaves gummed and blackening in the blood.

Kling was looking now at this object that the stone had rolled aside to reveal. There was no stone weighting him any more as he watched the object, feeling the bed shake under him as he shook and the muscles twitching in his forearms and thighs.

Then watching the object, while his heart pounded, he saw the hairs sprouting in his father's nostrils as he lay dead on the wooden bed that was like a wagon without wheels, he saw a movement detach itself from this man in the gully, or perhaps it was the torn shirt which flapped in the wind, only there was no wind, and he did not stop to investigate but, knowing only the obsessional urge to hide at all costs that which ought not to be exposed to the level light, hoisted his spade and shoved and battered and fought the topheavy rock until he heard a grinding crash and knew the torn face bashed out of sight, shapeless-smashed and hidden under the stone: and was it the same stone that burst his own chest and sank its black, dead heaviness in his heart?

The weight fell again now so that there was no more pain or fright and the bed did not shake; there was only the waiting that was nothingness really, and the men in blue talking and moving about the ward.

That was all that he knew, sweat slowly drying as he lay on the bed, and the old man buried mercifully by the stone. The others took no notice of Kling nor he of them and he heard their talk and did not know that he heard until a woman's voice cut through sharp, 'Williams, and the rest of you, why are you hanging about in the ward?' He turned his head then to the nurse who had just come in; she was speaking to him too: 'Kling, you're to go to Dr. Pope after tea. You'd better get up and make yourself decent', and he saw her pale, cold eyes linger on him as she went out of the door.

'Get up and make yourself decent,' the man called Williams said. 'That's a way to talk to a fellow who's sick.'

Kling said nothing but looked up at him, waiting.

'To hell with them,' Williams said. 'To hell with the whole set-up. Bloody racket to get sick men back into the army. Cannon fodder, that's all they care about. Taking advantage of poor mugs like us. Pep talks. Pills to pep you up. Dope to make you talk. Putting chaps to sleep and giving them electric shocks and Christ knows what. Lot of bloody guinea pigs, that's what we are. Bloody, isn't it?'

Kling was staring at him with blank eyes.

'Look at Kling here,' Williams said. 'Any fool can see he's as sick as hell. Why can't they leave him in peace? Why should he go back into their bloody army? This isn't his country anyway. Why should he fight for it?'

From the far reaches of his non-being Kling looked at the faces round him. They were all looking at him but they had no meaning. Williams had no meaning any more than the others. But he heard Williams go on.

'Damned gestapo methods. Spying and snooping around listening to talk. Bitches of nurses. Why the hell do we stand for it?'

A bell was ringing and the patients started to move out of the ward. Kling, staring up, saw the shapes of their meaningless faces receding from him. He looked at Williams who was still there and Williams looked back at him, smiling, and said, 'Coming to tea, chum?' And in the words Kling half recognized something forgotten and long-lost, and some corresponding thing in him which had died long ago almost revived itself; but the stone was too heavy for that resurrection, and he could not know that what he wanted to do was to smile.

'So long, then, if you're stopping here,' Williams said. He pulled a packet of Weights out of his pocket and put a cigarette on the bed beside Kling's hand which did not move. 'Don't let that bastard of a doctor put anything over on you', Kling heard Williams, walking towards the door, call back to him as he went.

Kling did not smoke the cigarette, or pick it up even; but after a time rose, and with those stiff motions which seemed to be rehearsing some exercise not well remembered, washed, dressed himself in shirt and blue trousers, combed his thick hair, and went along corridors to the door upon which was fastened the doctor's name.

There was a bench outside the door, and he sat down on it, waiting. The passage was dark because the windows had been coated with black paint for the blackout. Nothing moved in the long, dark, silent passage at the end of which Kling sat alone on the bench. He sat there bending forward, his hands clasped between his knees, his red tie dangling, his eyes fixed on the ground. He did not wonder what would happen behind the door. He waited, without speculation or awareness of waiting. It was all the same to him, outside or here or in the ward, he did not notice, it made no difference to his waiting.

A nurse opened the door and called him and he got up and stepped forward, and looking past her along the wall of the corridor thought, How many stones there are in this place; so many faces and stones: and lost the thought before it meant anything and went into the room.

'I want you to lie on the couch,' Dr. Pope told him. 'We're going to give you a shot of something that will make you feel a bit sleepy. Quite a pleasant feeling. It won't hurt at all.'

Obedient, null, with that unnatural stiffness, Kling laid himself down.

Lying on the high couch he looked at the exuberant ceiling without surprise. The flowers and the crowding cherubic faces did not seem any more strange to him than anything else. The ceiling did not concern him any more than the doctor concerned him. Nothing concerned him except the heaviness in his breast. He waited, looking at the doctor as if he had never seen him before, the nurse busy with swab and spirit and tourniquet, and he felt far off on his arm the tourniquet tightening, the bursting pressure of flesh against tightening fabric, and then the small sharp sting as the needle entered the vein.

'Just try to relax,' the doctor said, watching, while the fluid in the hypodermic went down, the blank waiting face with wide-open extremely dilated eyes.

He smiled his professional smile of encouragement, and looked from the face to the chest and the massive shoulders bulked rigid under the white shirt that they stretched tight, at the clenched strong hands, the rough blue cloth strained on the tensed thighs, the stiffly upthrust boots not neatly laced, and back to the blank face again. He noticed on the face how the deep tan of the outdoor years was starting to turn yellowish as it slowly faded inside hospital walls.

'Well, how do you feel now?' he asked, smiling, the man who stared up at him without answering.

'I want you to talk, Kling,' he said. 'I want you to tell me what's worrying you.'

Kling, his patient, looked away from him and up at the ceiling.

'What is it you've got on your mind?' asked the doctor.

Kling stared upwards without speaking and now his limbs started twitching a little.

'You'll feel better after you've talked,' Dr. Pope said.

The nurse finished the long injection and withdrew the syringe adroitly. A single drop of blood oozed from the pierced vein and she dabbed a shred of cotton wool on to it and silently carried her paraphernalia into the background and stood watching.

'You've got to tell me what's making you miserable,' the doctor said, speaking loud. He bent down and put his hand on Kling's shoulder and said loudly and very distinctly, close to his ear, 'You are very miserable, aren't you?'

Kling looked at him with his wide, black, lost animal's eyes and felt the hand on his shoulder. His shoulder twitched and something inside him seemed to be loosening, he felt sick in his stomach, and a sleepy strangeness was coming up at him out of nowhere, turning him tired, or sick.

'Why are you miserable?' he heard the question. 'Something happened to you, didn't it? Something you can't forget. What was that thing?'

Kling saw the doctor standing far too close, bending down almost on top of him. The hand that had hold of his shoulder gripped hard like a trap, the distorted face looked monstrous, foreshortened and suspended beneath painted faces, the eyes glaring, the threat of the mouth opening and shutting. Kling groaned, turning his head from one side to the other to escape from the eyes, but the eyes would not let him go. He felt the strangeness of sleep or sickness or death moving up on him, and then something gave way in his chest, the stone shifted, and sleep came forward to the foot of the

62

couch, and he groaned again, louder, clutching his chest, crumpling
the shirt and the red tie over his breastbone.

'Was it something bad that was done to you?' he heard the
doctor's voice shout in his ear.

He felt himself turning and twisting on the hard bed, twisting
away from the eyes and the voice and the gripping hand that was
shaking him now. He shut his eyes to escape, but a salt prick of
tears or sweat forced them open, he did not know where he was or
what was happening to him, and he was afraid. He was very
frightened with the strange sleep so near him, he wanted to call for
help, it was hard for him to keep silent. But somewhere in the midst
of fear existed the thought, They've taken everything; let them not
take my silence. And the queer thing was that Williams was somehow a part of this, his smile, the cigarette, and what he had spoken.

'Was it something bad that *you* did?' Kling heard.

He did not feel the hand that was shaking his shoulder. He only
felt his face wet, and on the other side of sleep a voice kept on
moaning while another voice shouted. But he could not listen because, just then, the stone moved quite away from his breast and
sleep came up and laid its languid head on his breast in place of
the stone.

He tried to look at the strange sleep, to know it, but it had no
form, it simply rested sluggishly on him, like gas, and all he could
see above was a cloud of faces, the entire earth was no graveyard
great enough for so many, nor was there room to remember a smile
or a cigarette or a voice any more.

The old man was there and had been for some time, not sprawled
in leaves now but standing, bent forward, listening; and Kling knew
that this time something must pass between them, there was something which must be said by him, in extenuation, or in entreaty, to
which the old man must reply: though what it was that had to
be said, or what words would be found to express it, did not
appear yet.

The old man bent over him and blood dripped on to his face and
he could not move because of what lay on his breast, and when the
old man saw he could not move he bent lower still and Kling could

see the tufts of bristly hairs in his father's nostrils. He knew he would have to speak soon, and, staring wildly, with the old man's face almost on his, he could see the side of the face that was only a bloodied hole and he heard a sudden frantic gasp and gush of words in his own language and that was all he heard because at that moment sleep reached up and covered over his face.

Dr. Pope and the nurse had both seen that Kling was going to start talking. The doctor had seen it coming for about half a minute and waited intently. The nurse looked expectant. When the first sounds came both of them had moved forward at once and the doctor had bent lower over his patient but now they stepped back from the couch.

'I was afraid that might happen,' Dr. Pope said in his impatient voice. 'Damned annoying. I suppose there's no one in the place who could translate?'

'I'm afraid not,' the nurse said.

'Exasperating,' the doctor said. 'So we shan't get anything out of him after all.'

'I'm afraid not,' the nurse said again.

'Most frustrating and disappointing,' said Dr. Pope. 'Oh, well, it's no good trying to work on him now.'

... 'in a culture which is completely disordered, prince and servant are enemies, old age and youth kill eachother, father and son bear cold hearts, brothers accuse eachother, the most intimate friends work against eachother, man and wife deceive eachother, ... day after day the danger increases ... the bonds of society are loosened ... the spirit becomes bestial ... the greed for gain grows ... duty and common sense arc forgotten. ...

Clouds appear in the shape of dogs, horses, white swans and columns of carriages ... Or they have the shape of a man in a blue garment and red head who does not move. His name is: the Heavenly Adversary ... or they have the shape of a host of horses fighting: those are called the Slaying Horses ... snakes crawl through the town from West to East ... horses and cattle begin to talk, dogs and pigs mate, wolves come into the city. Men fall from the sky ... When such signs appear in the land and its master does not better his ways in his fear, God shall send misfortune, sorrow and plague ... all kinds of death, annihilation, earthquake, destruction and grief shall arrive ... all this is caused by disorder in the state. ...'

LIE BU WE — about 300 B.C.

WHY did he leave me, I wonder? It seems almost incredible that less than a week has passed — only a few days, in fact — since I was preparing an evening meal for us both in this very room. How happy we were that evening. Or perhaps I ought to say, How happy I was: for events have turned out so differently from my expectations that I feel more than ever astray in the world, as though all my life I had been working along lines that had no relation at all to reality. When appearances prove so deceptive, one's own sensations are all that one really has to rely on; and I can say, at least, without any doubt, that I was extremely happy that evening.

It was, perhaps, the second or third meal we had eaten together in the little house; the house to which I had moved on purpose to be in the same district of the city as this auburn stranger who had dropped into my life as if from the clouds, bringing with him a happiness I had not expected to feel again.

It seemed such a gay little house then, with its yellow shutters, its steep ladder-like flight of stairs, and its small, oddly-shaped rooms, each one painted a different colour. There was the living-room all pale green like the springtime trees beneath which we walked every day after my work was finished; the bedroom coloured like almond blossom; the kitchen blue and white like one of those plates on which one traced as a child endless magic journeys.

I see that I have written in the past tense as if these rooms I'm describing no longer existed: and yet here I am, in that same blue and white kitchen where I was so happily preparing our meal that evening only the other day, when he said to me casually: 'Some time you will write about this because all that is beautiful must triumph for all.'

And I answered (I remember that I was taking an earthenware dish out of the oven at the moment and thinking more about that than about what I was saying), I answered: 'Yes, when it is all over between us, then I suppose I shall write down what I remember because nothing else of you will be left to me.'

The outward aspect of the house is still precisely the same as it was when those words were spoken. The paint is still fresh on the walls, the yellow shutters still present a frivolous brightness to the passers-by. It is only the character of the place which in this short time has become altogether different. Its personality has changed. It is not gay any longer. Oh, no, certainly gaiety has no connection whatever with these coloured walls which surround me with their implacable reminder of lost joy. Outer appearances remain un-altered, but the spirit which inspired every form with meaning has vanished, leaving only a shell behind.

When I look round at my few possessions, each one of which carries inextricably in its essence some amusing or tender associa-tion, I feel as though I were confronting a dear relative, perhaps a

66

brother, whose brain a sudden tragedy had unhinged. Everything is the same; the features, the figure, the hair: only the one vital element is missing without which the human being has no significance, no entity, no individual soul.

I have never heard of anybody who loved a mad person. I should think it would be impossible to do so. Pity or aversion one would feel, but not love. And the feelings I have for this house are a blend of aversion and pity, exactly as they would be for someone very close to me whose personality had deteriorated until there finally remained no more possibility whatever of contact between us.

Sometimes it is almost horror that comes over me at the sight of these rooms, these objects, for which the whole *raison d'être*, as it were, has been taken away. Why do these walls still stand? When every day and night, all over the city, buildings are being struck down, why does this house remain intact? How can it so obstinately fail to disintegrate, seeing that it no longer has any chance of fulfilling the purpose for which I first decided to occupy it?

Yes, it's just as if one were forced to live with someone out of his mind, or, worse still, with the actual physical corpse of a loved person which a diabolical chemistry had rendered immune from the process of dissolution.

The words with which I began writing, the words, 'Why did he leave me?' keep recurring to me although I try to drive them away. What's the use of tormenting myself with speculations about this man, dressed always in blue, whose arrival I did not witness and who departed in silence and unobserved? It is only necessary for me to know that he has gone, that he is far away, and that he will not return. Suddenly he left me, without warning or explanation, without saying good-bye. If I had known his intention that evening, could I have said or done anything to influence his decision? That is a question I often vainly consider, alone in these rooms which now have no meaning for me.

And why indeed should one expect to find a meaning in walls, in windows, or in a book that is not to be found on the shelf? In a city where everything is chaotic and inexplicable and where one is constantly beset by all kinds of death, annihilation, destruction and grief it is something, at all events, to be able to say: 'On that evening', or 'On such and such a day, I was happy'.

I've tried hard to solve the bitter riddle which brought me across the world to this place of misfortune when all I wished was freedom to live in peace, in sunshine, in a country where birds had not learnt to fly in terror from the sound of a falling bomb. Lately I've been thinking that possibly all these happenings are bound up together. That perhaps the man in the blue suit with whom I was happy, the man who left me so abruptly and, as it superficially appears, so unkindly, perhaps he was, in some obscure way, connected with my sentence; or even came with the express purpose of putting into my hands a clue which, if properly followed, would finally lead to the truth and make clear the justice of all these catastrophes which have fallen upon me.

How otherwise than as an unfulfilled obligation, and therefore as an indictment, can I translate that phrase of his, which at the time passed almost unnoticed, but which now seems to me to be the crux of the whole matter: 'All that is beautiful must triumph for all'?

THE BROTHER

Now that those days are as dead as the grave and I have so much time on my hands I feel a great and persistent need to record something of the relationship between myself and my brother. And the fact that I'm allowed to do so (indeed, I'm even encouraged to write by the provision of pencils and, in spite of the paper shortage, of plenty of cheap foolscap paper) makes me believe that perhaps those better able to judge than I have discerned in the long, submerged struggle between the two of us an example which may prove valuable to other people in the same sort of unfortunate circumstances.

There's plenty of time now to think back. Plenty of time to remember, to contemplate, to reflect on the disconnected, small, distant pictures which go to compose the whole gloomy canvas.

Sitting here in this lonely little room, without friends, without a future, without even a dream; sitting here hour after hour, listening to the sea's curious muffled bass which incorporates at irregular intervals a voice-like contralto pleading, I've arrived at certain decisions. I've decided to make a kind of précis, not a detailed analysis because that's beyond my powers, but a brief sketch of the pattern which my brother and I traced out in our mutual reactions. I'm not doing this in the hope of any amelioration of my own position (that I fully realize is out of the question and I don't even desire it); nor because I am inspired by an altruistic wish for others to profit by my misfortune; but simply because I want to get things clear in my own mind, and the best way to get things clear is to get them all written down.

To begin at the very beginning: I am the elder brother by two years. My birthday is in the spring, under the sign of Mars, and on that day, while I was at home, I was always accustomed to see my mother fill the vases with tulips like stiff fairy lights.

My brother was born in the dead of winter. I remember my mother telling us about the exceptional severity of that winter and

69

how the fountain in the square opposite our home spouted glittering sprays of ice instead of water, and the sparrows were found in dozens frozen to death. I remember particularly how she told us that somebody (I think it was one of the doctors at the hospital where she was confined), suddenly opening a door into the street, felt something crunch under his boot and discovered a little pile of dead birds which must have fluttered into the doorway for shelter before they became numbed.

The thought of those small, crushed, rigid bodies, which I picture as finches, is associated with early memories of my brother.

My brother. Ah, now I really grasp the difficulty of what I have undertaken. When it comes to the point of describing him my thoughts falter and turn aside. It's not that I don't remember him clearly, so much too clearly. But the act of concentration is like something unlawful. It's as if I were profanely trying to exhume his actual buried corpse. It's as if my brain cells themselves rejected a forbidden task. I begin to hesitate; I find myself listening attentively to the sea as if those never quite audible voices out there might be about to give me a message. But however closely I pay attention to the sea noise I can't distinguish anything definite: only the subdued, interminable clamour which now sounds to me like a high wind in the trees near the house where we used to live.

My brother. Slowly, slowly, his likeness comes in front of my eyes. Yet it isn't a distinct image of him even now. It isn't one picture so much as a series of pictures, taken at different ages and in different places, dissolving into one another and correspondingly vague. A white skin, red cheeks, chestnut hair. His skin was so white that you might have thought it a gift from the ice flowers on the window that witnessed his birth. People used to tease him by saying that such a beautiful white skin was wasted on a boy and should have belonged to a girl. He was big and strong though, not in the least girlish, and that was the reason, I suppose, that he didn't mind the teasing; that, and the gay, good-natured way that he had. It's his hair that I can remember most clearly; a wonderful head of rich red-brown curls with a lovely golden sheen, as glossy and fine as silk. If I'd been a girl I think I would have loved to run my fingers through his hair and unwind the curls which would, I'm sure, have briskly sprung back as soon as I let them go. I never did touch my brother's hair: and somehow this seems a sad thing to me. I think I could bear remembrance more easily if, even if only once, I had put my hand on his head.

My mother sometimes used to caress him in this way; but not frequently: not, at any rate, when I was present. Sometimes when we were all together in the evening I would notice her eyes turning fondly to his head bowed over a book. And I had the impression that she would have reached out to stroke his hair which shone so handsomely under the lamp if she had not been afraid of making me jealous or of hurting my feelings.

Poor mother. How she must have regretted the difference between her two sons. Even in the circumstances of our births we were totally different, and all her suffering and anxiety were on my account.

My brother came into the world easily in the glow of a frosty sunrise. From babyhood he was healthy and lovable and never caused a moment's alarm. Whereas I, dragged bloodily through a long and difficult birth, for years swung between life and death, the victim of an endless sequence of illnesses and accidents. All through my unlucky childhood my hold on life was precarious, and it was not until I was fully grown that my body appeared to reconcile itself more or less to the earth.

I have read the psychologists' theory that children born in springtime are liable to a lack of robustness because of the tension accumulating in the natural world during their term of embryonic development. But at the time when I was growing up children born in spring and summer were generally supposed to possess the pleasant characteristics of those seasons. Friends used to express surprise that I, with my auspicious birthday, was continually ailing, while my brother, who should have been handicapped by his freezing introduction to life, was a perfect model of mental and physical health.

Naturally, I could not fail to be aware of the comparisons which were made between the two of us, of course always in my disfavour.

My brother was tall, well-developed and fine to look at with his vivid colouring; kind, friendly, intelligent. I was puny, weak, incapable of tying my own shoelace without gasping for breath, my complexion was sallow, my hair stringy and dull, my manner lifeless or boorish and petulant.

When my brother brought friends to the house I would hide unsociably in my room. Or, worse, I would sit among them like a malicious goblin, damping their high spirits with my sneers and silences and bitter remarks.

In this way, as time went on, a gradual alienation took place for which I was entirely to blame. Up to the very end my brother was always considerate, gentle, eager to make friends with me. My heart sinks with shame and remorse now when I remember how often when he came back from his work in the business part of the town he would sit at home, trying to coax me into a good mood with his amusing talk, instead of spending the evening with his companions. How patient he was, and how little response he got from me. As likely as not I would try to pick a quarrel with him for his pains. But he would never be goaded into hostility, and if he saw that I was determined to stick to my bad temper, he would simply sigh and go out of the room; not reproachfully, but with such a sad, disappointed look that my heart almost breaks when I recall it.

And my mother. I see that I have hardly written anything about her as yet, although she was so much the centre of both our lives. Our father died when I was only a few years old and I have no recollection of him at all. My first memories are all of my mother, bending over me, stroking me with cool hands, holding a cup to my lips, soothing me through the mazy fevers of interminable nights, taking me for precious outings during my rare spells of comparative health. She was gay and pretty in those early days, smiling often, and singing, and with a quaint humour distinctively hers. That is the way I like to remember her. As a girl she must have been charming, with my brother's bright hair and complexion. I used to hear people say when we were children how much he resembled her.

It hurts me to think that it was the strain of looking after me which dimmed her brightness prematurely. Her devotion to me was extraordinary. At the time I took it for granted, never having known what it was to be left without her care for a single day. But now I realize that there was something fanatical, almost abnormal, in her determination to keep me alive and to shield me from every blow. There was even — how can I convey what I mean? — a touch of perversity in her protectiveness. I hardly know how to express it except by saying that her will for my welfare exceeded the natural bounds of maternal love and assumed a masochistic quality.

For my sake, although she was still a young and attractive woman, she sacrificed all social amusements. Because I was an invalid and could seldom go out, and then only for short periods, we lived a life of almost complete seclusion. When my brother started to earn his living and to bring his friends to the house I noticed a brief revival of her vitality. She looked younger, and began to speak again in the old humorous way that she had abandoned. Even her hair seemed to become more alive although its colour had faded.

But the pleasure of seeing these young people she also renounced on the grounds that their presence disturbed me. It would be best, she decided, that my brother should not invite his friends to our home since I was always upset by them and thrown into a state of quarrelsome agitation by their talk.

Not long after this the one-sided conflict between us intensified and it became apparent that I could not or would not agree with my brother even on the few occasions that we were together. A sort of frenzy of malice entered into me at this time. I was jealous of his looks, of his popularity, of the fact that he played his part in the world as an effective member of society while I was forced to drag out a wretched existence lying on sofas in darkened rooms. To my jealousy was added a devastating sense of inferiority. And these two emotions working together like deadly germs in the blood generated an uncontrollable aggression against my brother which broke out in constant violent and utterly unjustified accusations.

He, acting no doubt on my mother's suggestion, spent less and less time with us. He still slept at home, but most of his days were passed elsewhere and often he did not come home until long after I had gone to bed.

My mother did not speak of him or of his lengthened absences. I, encased in my own egotism, was happy in her even more undivided attention and pleased myself with the thought that her pleasure equalled mine.

We now lived a life restricted to tiny domestic details. I rested on the sofa and read and on good days pottered about out of doors. My mother attended to the house and cooked the special foods which she never allowed anyone else to prepare for me. This time she seemed definitely and finally to have turned away from her youth. Her hair began to go grey. She became very silent; not melancholy, but certainly not gay; and though her manner towards me was quietly cheerful her smile seldom appeared. Sometimes I would catch her sitting listlessly like a quite old woman, and I would wonder at the change that had taken place in one who used to be lively and whimsical. I do not say that I was perturbed by the change. In a way it even caused me a feeling of complacency as though she had become more wholly mine by giving up everything else.

All that concerned me was that we were alone and always together and that nothing interfered with the cloud of protection in which she enveloped me.

Now comes the part that is hardest of all to set down. I feel my brain starting to spin, and I must hurry on before confusion engulfs me completely.

It was bitterly cold weather and I was recovering from an attack of influenza. My brother had caught the infection from me, but mildly, and had been at home in bed for two or three days.

On his first day downstairs the two of us were in the study where most of my existence was passed, I on my usual sofa, he in an armchair by the fire. It was a long while since we had been in the same room together for more than a few minutes at a time. As we rested there, both with our books, I was conscious of him glancing at me now and again as if there were something he wanted to say. Contrarily, I refused to take any notice for several minutes, but when I finally looked up I met his eyes gazing eagerly and wistfully into mine.

As soon as he saw that I was looking at him he got up, put his book aside, and came over to me. Standing beside the sofa, looking down with that candid smile that was so hard to resist, he began to speak to me in a gentle, appealing voice, saying how sorry he was that we had drifted so far apart, begging my pardon if he had hurt me in some way, and asking if we could not make an effort to get on better together, if only for mother's sake.

He spoke so earnestly and with such simple friendliness and good-will that I felt a sudden softening towards him. O God, how much I really wanted to yield myself up to him then, to tear out my black heart and throw it down at his feet. I wanted to love him and to be loved in return. What would I not have given for the power to respond when his hand came down affectionately on my shoulder.

But at that very moment an awful seizure gripped hold of me, my head felt as though it must burst open, and, as if to relieve the intolerable congestion of the brain, a tremendous paroxysm of coughing came on, shaking me so viciously that the walls of my chest seemed to be torn apart.

My brother tried to support me in my convulsions. I can still see his face, a little pale after illness, abruptly turning whiter with shock and dismay. My mother came running with medicine in a glass, but I was too far gone to drink. Accustomed to these crises, she at once knew what to do. There was a certain ampoule that, when crushed, exhaled a vapour which gave me relief: but by an unusual oversight there were none of these in the house. At once she prepared to run to the druggist who lived not far away. I, however, as soon as I realized her intention, held her back, clutching her hand, and indicating as well as I could in the midst of my spasms that she was not to leave me.

I'll go, my brother offered immediately, already on his way to the door.

But you shouldn't go out in this cold, my mother said. You're not well yourself yet.

Even in my extremity I saw the agonized look that she gave him with those words, and felt her hand jerk in mine.

Let him go, I tried to say. It won't hurt him. He's so strong. I don't know if I actually spoke aloud. At any rate, he was gone.

My mother made no further protest. In silence she did what she could for me, easing my acute distress until the ampoule was brought. Later on I was helped to bed, none the worse for the dreadful fit.

Next day my brother was seriously ill with pneumonia. By the evening he was delirious; unconscious the following day. Just before the end he came to himself. My mother fetched me from the place where I was lying prostrated with sorrow and a kind of dread impossible to describe in words.

You must come, she said. He is asking for you.

I did not want to go to the bedside. I was afraid.

Come, my mother said in a stern voice I had never heard. He is dying.

Trembling, I followed her to the room.

I believe some relatives were there as well as the doctor, but I did not see them. I saw only my brother, propped up with pillows, and changed. His short fatal illness had changed him exceedingly. His face had turned sunken and sallow, his hair had lost its gloss and stuck to his forehead in dank strands. Violent tremors shook me as I stood at the side of the bed. Was it my own or my brother's dying face that confronted me there, distorted by anguished breaths?

I saw that he wished to say something to me and stooped over him. The fearful sound of his breathing was so loud that it seemed to be inside my head. I had the sensation of participating in the agony of a man being tortured to death, and my shudders became so uncontrollable that I was afraid of falling upon him. At last words came; clear, and yet not like human speech at all, they came from so far away.

It's a pity.

It was like listening to a voice speaking across oceans and continents. And after a long delay, very softly, so that none of the others heard, followed two more words.

For you.

I don't know what happened then. I only remember the terrible pang that pierced through my whole being, the consciousness of some priceless thing irrevocably lost, as if a vital organ had been ripped out of my body.

I have a dim impression of confused commotion, of a lamentable cry, of the doctor hurrying forward. Was it I or my mother who cried out and fell on the bed? I'm not certain. All I know is that my brother was dead and that someone supported me from the room.

Later on, perhaps many hours later, I was lying again on my sofa. It was night time. A light burned on the table under a heavy shade. I think I must have been given a sedative, for I seemed to climb laboriously up a million steps from the depths of uneasy sleep. For a long time I lay absolutely still, staring at the circle of light on the tablecloth. The cloth was one of those thick old-fashioned affairs, coloured a deep blue, and I looked at it with the disinterested attention one might give to a rare object one had not seen before. By doing this I managed partially to insulate myself from reality. I was aware and yet unaware of the tragedy that had happened.

At last my mother came into the room. I did not look at her. Always before when she had opened the door I had turned towards her with confident and eager expectation of comfort. But now I did not want to see her. I did not want to raise my eyes from the tablecloth. I felt myself starting again to tremble as I had done at my brother's deathbed: long, deep inward shudders ran over my secret nerves.

My mother said nothing. I was aware that she had come into the middle of the room and was standing beside the table. I had the idea that she was waiting for me to speak some particular word, but what it might be I could not imagine. Very slowly and with the greatest possible reluctance I lifted my eyes.

She was standing looking down at me, resting one hand on the table. It seemed to me that something about her was different: not the black dress, because for a long time now she had habitually worn black; nor her pallor, although I noticed that her face was unusually white. It was rather that something indefinable seemed to have been taken from her.

The silence between us became intolerable and I stammered something intended for consolation, saying that at least we still had each other.

Yes, you are all that is left now, she said in a low, grave tone, while her eyes appeared to be studying me with the same unnatural and dispassionate consideration that I had bestowed on the table-cloth.

And suddenly, as she stood there looking at me so quietly and steadfastly in the quiet room, at night, with the lamp burning, the terrible revelation sprang out like writing upon the wall, and I realized everything, my own blindness, the horror. It was not I but my brother whom my mother had loved all along. He was the treasure of which I had robbed her for all these years and of which I had now deprived her for ever.

As if she knew what was in my mind she remarked:

You were always stronger than he was, and now you have managed to get rid of him for good.

A blue thread from the tablecloth had caught on her sleeve, and as she was speaking she carefully picked it off and threw it away. I don't know why, but this little action of hers was more than I could endure, and I groaned and hid my face in my hands.

I suppose she must have gone out of the room then although I did not hear her go. But after a minute the most awful thing of all happened: I heard her voice crying from the staircase in that dreadful, inhuman tone of a person screaming out of a nightmare, O, what will become of us now?

Whatever happens to me, I shall never forget that terrible cry. No walls, however high and thick, can exclude it. Nothing that I could possibly be called upon to bear could drown that sound which is always in my ears now like an accompaniment to the waves breaking outside.

What will become of us now? For her you might say the question is finally answered. And yet, was the answer really contained in that narrow box that so soon after my brother's coffin took the same steep journey down the dark stairs of our home? When the barber comes round and sets up his glass I look at my reflection and wonder whether the whole drama is not still going on here, in this little room, inside these high walls. Perhaps there will never be an end to it at all. Or perhaps the end will only come when no mirror reflects me any more. Perhaps when I die, perhaps death alone will bring peace, the armistice and end to this sad internecine strife.

THE GANNETS

It was springtime, a windy day. I had walked a long way on the cliffs by a path that I did not know. Gannets were diving like snow falling into the sea, pursuing a shoal of fish that kept parallel with the shore. I'm not certain now whether I walked so far in order to watch the gannets or to explore the coast, or simply because it was a bright afternoon.

After winding for a long time between low bushes and rocks, the path suddenly began to climb steeply over a headland. Seeing the difficult track ahead made me realize that I was tired, and that I had already come much further than I had intended. From the position of the sun I knew that it must be getting late. The sensible thing would have been to turn back then: especially as the gannets, which I had perhaps been following unconsciously, were vanishing round the rocky point shaped like the snout of a huge saurian. But instead of starting the long walk home I kept on, telling myself that I might as well see what lay beyond the head since I had come so far. It was quite a stiff climb, the path was slippery with pine needles and loose stones, and I was breathless by the time I got to the top. There was nothing about the view from the crest, either, to justify the effort of getting there. However far I looked I could see only a vista of the same yellowish rocky cliffs topped with pine trees and scrub which had been in front of my eyes the whole afternoon.

A few yards away, in a hollow of the downward slope, was a dilapidated wooden shack. At first I thought it must be some old boat-shed or deserted fisherman's hut. The half-ruined place, apparently only held together by roughly nailed boards and wire and patched with beaten-out tins, seemed much too ramshackle to be inhabited. But then I saw signs of occupancy: a heap of fresh potato peelings thrown outside the door, a few indescribably sordid rags hanging from the crazy posts of what had once been a fence.

I stood there in the wind for a minute, resting and getting my breath after the climb. And as I was wondering how any human being could be so unfortunate or so degraded as to live in such squalor, five or six children appeared and clustered together staring out to sea: they were, like the hovel, indescribably squalid, almost naked, hideous with neglect. They pointed towards the sea where the gannets on this side of the point were diving much closer in, with folded wings hurtling like bolts through the air, to strike the water one after the other in jets of spray. I could not hear much of what the children were saying, but it seemed from certain words and from their gestures that they expected the birds to come near. I waited to see what would happen. We all gazed at the gannets which were now no longer diving or searching the waves but planing portentously towards us with infrequent wing strokes. And sure enough I was presently half-deafened by a storm of harsh cries immediately overhead. Long black-tipped wings hid the sun, shadowing everything; only the cold round eyes and the fierce beaks glittered. And hardly had the flock sighted the children than they seemed to be menacing them, screaming headlong towards them in horrid haste. I shouted some sort of warning, urging the children to run into the house. They took no notice. I saw their looks full of excitement and anticipation, but without any amazement. They seemed to be taking part in a procedure well known to them. Already the gannets were swooping upon one of them, the smallest of the group, whom two of the others dragged along by her stick-like arms. And it was beyond all possibility of doubt that this miserable little creature was the victim among them, already dedicated to the birds. Not terror alone gave such a shocking blankness to her lifted face, darkened by two great holes, bloodied pits from which the eyes had already been torn. I shouted again and began running with an idea of beating the gannets off with my hands; but then I must have stumbled and fallen heavily. I must have been stunned by the fall on the jagged rock, for when I got up the cliff was silent and lonely, the wind had died down, and the sun was sinking behind sullen bars of cloud edged with fire.

How did all this atrocious cruelty ever get into the world, that's what I often wonder. No one created it, no one invoked it: and no saint, no genius, no dictator, no millionaire, no, not God's son himself, is able to drive it out.

THE PICTURE

THE sun was shining the afternoon I went for the picture. Of course there wasn't anything very remarkable about that because the sun does shine more here in the winter than it does at home. But that afternoon it shone as if the winter had almost come to an end; as if the very next day, perhaps, might be the first day of spring.

How hard winter is to bear in a foreign country, even when there is sunshine. The cold mornings open their eyes to glare at you one after another, like hostile strangers. Everything will be easier when the spring comes, I used to say to myself whenever I was confronted with one of those difficult situations or problems which are certain to arise so often in a strange environment.

Walking along the street on this day that I'm talking about I was happy to feel the spring close at hand. The town, which generally has rather a drab appearance, for once looked quite gay. Flags were blowing over some of the buildings, there was a breezy seaside liveliness in the air, flocks of gulls with bright scarlet legs and beaks followed some laughing girls who threw them the remains of the lunch they had been eating in the public gardens.

The pleasure which I got from seeing these things added itself to the pleasure I felt about the picture I was going to fetch from the shop. It was a week since I had taken it there to be framed, and all through the week I had been thinking how happy I should be when the time came to hang it up on the wall, an ally in the alien territory of my room.

The old man to whom the shop belonged had promised to have the picture framed ready for me to-day. As I went along I remembered with gratitude his aspect of a benevolent gnome and the kindly way he had interested himself in the picture and advised me about the most suitable style of frame. Since I've travelled so far afield I've learned to be cautious; I know that it doesn't do to attach one's hopes to anybody or to indulge in what's called wishful thinking, but in this case I felt safe enough; I felt sure the old man would not disappoint me.

The shop was on the shady side of the street, and when I crossed over from the other pavement where I'd been walking I was surprised at the difference in temperature between the shade and the sun. The inside of the shop felt really chilly, and it was dark as well, so that for the first few moments after I'd come through the door I thought the place was quite empty. Tradesmen in this part of the world have a habit of leaving their shops unattended if business is slack, and there's usually a hand-bell on the counter which a customer rings as he comes in to attract attention. It wasn't until after I'd rung the bell, which in this case was an uncommon one made of glass, that I saw there was somebody already in the shop. A man of medium height, rather thin, wearing a long coat like an ulster and a nondescript hat, was standing with his back towards me, apparently studying some prints fastened to a tall screen near the door. I can't attempt to explain the impression I got then, an impression that was absolutely illogical and contradicted by the man's very attitude as he stood, turned away from me and bending forward slightly as if straining his eyes in the dim light to examine the pictures before him: the impression that he was, if not actually watching me, at any rate acutely conscious of my arrival.

It's not exactly agreeable to feel that a stranger has got you under observation, particularly if you happen to be a long way from home in a place where things frequently turn out quite different from what they appear. My optimistic mood began to evaporate, I was disappointed, too, because the person who answered the bell was not the old man whom I'd been expecting and upon whom, for some reason, I seemed to have pinned my faith, but a dark-haired girl in a red dress whom I'd never seen before. As she came in I looked at the man near the door, supposing that he would be attended to first since he had arrived before me. But he did not turn or change his position in any way, nor did the girl even glance at him. There seemed to be some understanding between them; obviously the man was not in the shop as an ordinary customer, and this was somehow disturbing to me although anticipation of seeing the picture was uppermost in my mind.

The girl asked what I wanted, and, as soon as I had told her, she

83

began to look at the labels on a number of brown paper packages that were leaning against the wall. Again I'm unable to explain the feeling which came over me while she was searching, the conviction that she was not looking seriously, that she did not really expect to find my picture among all those brown paper parcels. If only the old man would come I'm sure he would be able to find it at once, I thought. But he did not appear and I felt myself helpless. The situation already seemed to have developed beyond my control. I was oppressed by an intuition, hard to put into words, that the true meaning of what was happening was in some way hidden from me: and yet I dreaded the moment when it would become clear.

The girl, after going through the wrapped pictures in an aimless way, picked one out, as it seemed to me, quite at random, and laid it on the counter. This will be yours, she said, apparently expecting me to accept it without further inquiry.

But it's got someone else's name written on it, I said, pointing at a word pencilled on the brown paper so indistinctly that I couldn't make out what it was but which contained far more letters than there are in my two names put together.

For the first time she gave me a faint smile. That's easily put right, she said. She took a piece of india-rubber out of her pocket and quickly erased the writing on the parcel. There you are, she said, pushing it towards me and moving away as if the whole business had been satisfactorily cleared up.

Wait a minute, I called after her. I must make sure that I've got the right one. I hurriedly started to undo the parcel, but the string was so securely tied that it took me some seconds to get it open. Just as I expected, it was not my picture inside, but an inane nursery print of a frog in a top hat. I pulled the paper back over the wretched thing. The mere sight of it was exasperating, and I remember feeling surprised at the sad tone in which I exclaimed, Of course this isn't mine. Why didn't my voice sound indignant?

The girl, who had just opened the door between the shop and a room at the back, looked at me with a blank face. The old man knows all about my picture, I said. Won't you please ask him to come here and speak to me? She didn't answer. I was afraid she was going to refuse. But then, still without speaking, she went out and shut the door between us.

Now I remembered uneasily the man behind me whose presence I had forgotten during the last few seconds. I glanced round casually, not wishing to give the impression that I felt any interest in him. At first I thought he must have gone away; but then I saw that he had merely moved to a darker corner where he was standing in exactly the same pose as before although, in such deep shadow, he could not possibly have distinguished a single detail of the pictures at which he seemed to be peering. So he really is watching me, passed through my head. And suddenly it occurred to me that it would be wise for me to leave the shop, immediately, without troubling any further about the picture.

I had actually taken a step towards the street door when the old man appeared from the inner room. At once I turned to him with relief, confident that he would be able to put everything right. I've come for my picture, I said to him. You remember. The picture you advised me about. It was to be ready to-day.

Picture? Picture? he repeated in an unexpectedly querulous voice, at the same time glancing impatiently from side to side as he came up to me. What picture? There are hundreds of pictures here.

I was so disconcerted that for a minute I simply stared at him. Then it began to dawn on me that the thing which has so often happened to me in this country had happened again, that I had made a mistake, that I had fallen into the trap of accepting as real an appearance that was merely a sham, a booby trap, a malicious trick. The old man was very near me and I could see his teeth yellow and broken and bad like rat's teeth under his ragged moustache, and his vindictive red-rimmed eyes gummy with rheum. How could I ever have thought he had a benevolent face? What a fool I was to be so easily taken in.

But you must remember my picture, I pleaded, not yet quite able, in spite of everything, to despair. Speaking with a contemptible note of propitiation I began to describe our previous interview, recalling what had been said on that occasion. The old man waited unwillingly. I could not tell whether he was even listening to me as he stood, glancing about, and thrusting a long black pencil in and out of a tuft of straggly hair just above his ear.

Yes, yes, he interrupted irritably in the end, and going once more to the door of the other room where I could now see an apprentice in a white apron at work at a table.

Perhaps it's in there, my precious picture, I thought. I no longer had the least trace of confidence in the old shopkeeper. I felt convinced, just as I had with the girl, that he had no intention of finding the picture, would not so much as look for it, even if he were not, as seemed only too probable, actually hiding it from me. If only I could go in and look round for myself perhaps I should see it somewhere, I was thinking, when he rudely shut the door in my face.

So strong was my desire for the picture that I think I might have tried to force my way into the room to hunt for it. And that in spite of the fact that I knew I ought to leave the shop at once, at that very moment, that I had stayed too long already. I think I would have chanced everything if the old man had not opened the door a crack just then and whispered, Perhaps you would be able to describe the picture to me? His face was close, much too close to mine, and I saw his mouth with its disgusting rat's teeth twisting into an indescribably sly and venomous sneer, while at the very same instant the man in the shop behind me, whose face I had not seen, uttered a sound that could only have been a suppressed laugh. Yes, they were both laughing. And I had no doubt about who was the victim of their cruel joke. The girl and the apprentice in the white apron were certainly having a good laugh, too, at my expense although I couldn't see or hear either of them from where I was standing.

I stumbled out of the place somehow. I was so humiliated, so disappointed, that I hardly knew what I was doing and turned in the wrong direction when I got into the street. The sun had stopped shining now, a dismal wind blew the dust in eddies presaging rain.

How terribly long and hard the winters seem when one is far from home.

ALL KINDS OF GRIEF SHALL ARRIVE

THINGS turn out so strangely and unexpectedly in one's life. If anybody had told me a few years back that people would be coming to me for information about the authorities I shouldn't have been able to help laughing. When one's a free agent nothing seems more fantastically improbable than the idea of being entangled with officialdom. Stories about those who get involved with the authorities don't seem to have a personal application at all; if anything, they strengthen one's sense of immunity. Those sort of things may happen to other people, I used to think; but not to me. I was inclined then to adopt a superior, slightly pitying, slightly contemptuous attitude towards unluckier individuals as if they had only themselves to blame for their troubles. In those days I hadn't yet learnt that the authorities are really not concerned with a person's motives or his private character or even with his public behaviour, and that somebody quite blameless (as we think) may easily become deeply implicated simply through a slight oversight or perhaps a technical error only due to a lack of information which is certainly not his fault.

The fact of the matter, of course, is that no one can be sure of avoiding trouble; the completely innocent person perhaps least of all; because he, unsuspicious, and lulled into a false sense of security by his clear conscience, is liable to overlook some little formality that may bring him under official notice. Just such a slip is all that's needed to set the ball rolling. Official procedure is always incalculable, but the one thing we can count on is that once a name has come before the authorities, in no matter how harmless a context, it will never be expunged from the records. A name appears, let us say, on some absolutely trivial pretext; perhaps even because of a civic action that would be accounted creditable by ordinary standards. Immediately the whole ponderous mechanism is engaged, countless wheels start to revolve, new ledgers are opened, documents are drawn up, in who knows how many different departments whole staffs of clerks set to work searching and correlating and noting and filing, until, in a surprisingly short time, a huge dossier is prepared. And from this dossier, which is constantly being revised and brought up to date, the subject can never hope to escape until his death. Some people go further still, and say that the dossier is extended to include the direct descendants of the original subject, so that anyone who has had a relative under observation is himself automatically suspect. Personally, however, I disagree with such an extreme view which, if correct, would implicate someone in practically every family.

It's the lack of reliable information about these matters and the crop of legends and superstitions that have grown out of ignorance which make a person who is, or who thinks he is likely to be, in trouble, turn to anybody who seems to have the least understanding of official affairs. That's why people have started coming to me; though heaven knows I can do little to help them. Certainly, during the last few years, I've had a great deal of experience in dealing with the authorities; and because, on the whole, things haven't gone entirely against me, a rumour has got round that I've evolved some specially successful technique of my own. In reality I'm convinced that any approach systematic enough to be called a technique would be far too rigid to stand a chance of success in dealing with the authorities whose reactions are essentially capricious, unpredictable and inconsistent. But this view is not readily acceptable to outsiders, obsessed as they are by the fantasy of official logic, and confused as well by the conflicting theories of their advisors.

But look here, they say to me: Surely there must be some hidden laws governing these obscure processes. Admittedly a lot of official business seems quite senseless and contradictory to us. But isn't it probable that behind it all there is an understandable formula which, once we have grasped it, will make order out of what previously looked like confusion? Shouldn't we really devote all our energies to a diligent search for such a key?

It's hard to give a satisfactory answer to this; and I sometimes think that an account of an actual case points a clearer moral than any amount of talk: as, for instance, A's Case.

I've known A nearly all my life. Latterly, since I've had so many dealings in official quarters, I've come to recognize certain distinguising marks in people who are doomed to trouble with the authorities. I don't mean to say that everyone who is going to get into difficulties will bear these characteristics: but any person who does possess them is sure to go through a bad time sooner or later. A always had these distinguishing signs very strongly marked; but in earlier, happier days I was not aware of their significance.

I still remember the morning A came to tell me that for some unimaginable reason she had received an official notification to appear before the authorities. It was a beautiful, still sunny day and quail were calling out from the heath up above my cottage. Seeing her standing beside the door, with her hair blowing about and her bewildered face anxious in sunshine, I thought what a sad thing it was when young people got caught up in our strange official system. Elderly and middle-aged people at least have their memories to sustain them in dark times; but someone like A, a quiet young woman fond of birds, has no such inner support.

Well, in due course the case came on, and it had the distinction of being terminated quite quickly instead of dragging along in the usual inconclusive, heartbreaking way. The details, of course, were never made public. All that became known was that a verdict had been obtained against A and that she had actually started to serve her sentence. The next thing we heard, and it certainly came as a surprise, was that she had left the country. I don't mean to imply that she had escaped. We all know such a thing is impossible. But it seemed odd, to say the least of it, that, right at the beginning of her sentence, the authorities should suddenly allow her to go abroad. When I first heard about it I concluded that she was, inexplicably, being handed over to the foreign authorities. Afterwards, when I heard A's own story of what happened, I found out that no apparent restriction of any kind was placed on her movements.

She told me that she herself (rather naively) thought she was being given a reprieve. Pardons are issued by our authorities so rarely, perhaps only once in a century, that most advisors will hardly bother to apply for one: but A in her youthful optimism persuaded herself that hers was the unique case chosen to receive leniency. It seems that an official of unknown rank simply walked in one afternoon and without any explanation whatever released her and returned her belongings. Later on when she had time to go through her baggage she found everything intact, even down to some scribbled notes she had slipped into her coat pocket on the day of the final hearing. At the bank, where she went uncertainly to see if she could cash a cheque, her account was still open; in fact, a quite considerable sum had been credited to her anonymously.

You may wonder why A didn't just go home and take up her life where she had left it, since no obstacle was placed in the way of her doing so. Put yourself in her position, though, for a minute. Imagine the stares, the whispers, the veiled tentative questions, the startled or morbidly inquisitive faces which she would certainly have to encounter day after day, at her work, in the street, at a restaurant — wherever she happened to go. Imagine her relations with her superiors who, though they would hardly take the responsibility of discharging her in such anomalous circumstances, would surely regard her with a good deal of disfavour, if not with downright suspicion. What chances would she have of ultimate promotion, of success in her chosen career? And then, setting aside purely material considerations, imagine how she would stand with her friends, some of whom would doubtless cold-shoulder her, while in the company of the others she would never feel really at ease because she would never know that their association with her might not be telling against them in official quarters, or that they themselves were not, out of pity or politeness or loyalty, concealing their true feelings towards her. When all these things are taken into account her decision to go abroad isn't very surprising.

Besides, A was young and without ties and she had money to spend. Here, she thought, was a good opportunity of seeing the world and at the same time escaping from unpleasant associations. She accepted the popular fallacy that the past can be cut off like a diseased limb by the simple method of travelling a great many miles away from its locale.

It seems that she considered the move a success. No one in the distant country could know anything about her, she was starting with a clean sheet, and for a whole year she lived there very contentedly. That is what she told me. But there is some doubt in my mind. This part of her story always seems thin and unreal, like a dream imperfectly recollected. Whenever I have questioned A about this period her replies have been strangely vague. Yes, yes, of course I was happy, she would say to me: I had got away from it all. But when I pressed her for details her thoughts seemed to wander, she would glance about restlessly, making aimless movements with her hands, and at the same time repeating, Yes, I was very happy; but in such a queer vague way that I felt still more dubious.

And how did you live? What did you do? What sort of friends did you have there? I used to go on, determined, if I could, to get something more definite out of her. But she never really answered these questions, just saying evasively that she hadn't done anything much, that she had lived out in the country, in an isolated place, and so had not had many chances of making friends. And then she would look awkward and become silent. And if I badgered her still further she would insist on changing the subject.

Not that I got the impression that A was concealing anything or misleading me purposely. It was rather that I felt as if she herself were uncertain; as if she couldn't remember properly what had happened; as if, perhaps, she half suspected that none of this really had happened. What was it that made her repeat over and over again in such a peculiar way the words, I was very happy then? Was it simply that what came afterwards was so much worse? Or was it a subconscious attempt to bolster up the belief that she had once, during that brief dreamlike period, actually escaped the supervision of the authorities?

For a year then, according to A's own words, she was happy in her new environment. It was a year after her arrival to the day that she received the official communication recalling her. A year to the day. How significant that is. If anything were needed to convince one that the case had never been shelved for a moment, it's just that typical instance of mechanical official routine. One can almost see some close, dismal office that is always gloomy because the windows are made either of frosted glass or glass that's so covered with dirt and cobwebs that it's no longer transparent; the walls dark with hundreds of files and ledgers; the clerks working at their desks, or, more likely, lounging and gossiping near the stove at the end of the room, totally indifferent to all the suspense and suffering and despair centered around them.

It must have been a dreadful shock to A to receive this message after a whole year of apparent security. And yet I wonder whether it really was such a surprise to her? Whether she had not been half expecting something of the sort all the time, and whether she was not, in some part of herself, almost glad when the blow actually fell?

The first thing she did was to hurry to the main seaport, which was not far away, to make arrangements for her return. People to whom she spoke on the journey were pessimistic about her chances of getting a passage. In fact, they seem to have done their best to discourage her by talking about the difficulty of obtaining a passport, the infrequent sailings, and the inadequate passenger accommodation, most of which was automatically reserved for the great numbers of officials who were always travelling about. It was a thoroughly bad start to a bad business, and A was most apprehensive when she arrived at her destination. But here everything turned out unexpectedly simple. Just as often happens when one anticipates insuperable difficulties, all obstacles mysteriously melted away. She entered the department where she had to make her first application feeling diffident and depressed and wondering what sort of treatment she would receive from the officials who doubtless knew all about her case. To her astonishment the whole affair went through with perfect smoothness and speed. The clerks in the outer office spoke politely to her and, instead of following their usual practice of whispering and tittering together while the visitor cools his heels helplessly on the other side of the barrier, they announced her at once.

The official before whom A was taken was a rather fat man of about forty with fair hair and a small moustache. His round, plump face gave him a genial look quite in keeping with his affable manner. He shook hands with A, offered her a chair and a cigarette, and assumed an attentive attitude while she was speaking. A noticed, however, that he didn't seem to be listening very carefully as his eyes were constantly straying back and forth between the papers spread out on his desk and his neat fingernails. Finally, before A's statement was half finished, the man cut her short, saying, So the fact of the matter is that you want to leave, eh? And as soon as possible, I presume. Well, you couldn't have chosen a luckier moment.

He got up then, clapped A on the back in the friendliest manner, and, still keeping his hand on her shoulder, led her to the window and pulled up the holland blind, revealing a fine view of the docks. The department was on the third floor of a big waterfront building and the various ships lying alongside the wharves could all be clearly distinguished. A must have been as interested as she was surprised by this sudden revelation of things which are generally kept so secret. The official pointed out a ship docked almost directly below. She's sailing to-night, he said; and as it happens there's just one berth still available.

One can imagine A's utter amazement, her stammered questions about the passport, the permits, the hundred and one different formalities she had been told. The official airily waved every-thing aside, remarking that it was a rush, certainly, but that there were occasions on which these things could be managed. He gave A a bundle of forms to fill up and the addresses of certain offices she would have to visit before leaving, shook hands with her again and walked with her to the door, smiling the whole while.

A passed the rest of the day in a turmoil of activity. The places at which she had to report were scattered all over the town, and though she did not meet with obstruction at any of them there was the inevitable waiting about and repetition and delay, so that she barely got everything done before closing time. It was quite dark, starting to rain, and the offices were all deserted when she finally reached the docks with her papers in order. Armed policemen at the gates examined her pass with their flashlights before admitting her, and a specially tall policeman at the head of the gangway took the pass from her as she came aboard.

A has told me that she was too tired and excited and bewildered to have a very clear recollection of what followed. And this isn't surprising in view of the fact that she was at once shown into a fairly large cabin, the captain's presumably, where a party was in full swing. There were eight or ten men packed into the cabin, which was so full of smoke that A could hardly distinguish their faces as she was introduced by one of the ship's officers who had somehow got hold of her name. She got a confused impression of people, all talking in loud tones and with glasses in their hands, some sitting, some standing, some in official or naval uniforms, some still wearing their mufflers and unfastened civilian greatcoats just as they had come in from outside: of a medley of charts, printed warnings, instructions and prohibitions, incongruously plastered over the walls among pictures of actresses and naked women. A, too, soon had a glass in her hand, and found herself jammed into a corner beside a large elderly man in a bright yellow golf jacket. Some minutes passed before she realized that this oddly dressed man, already a little drunk, was the ship's captain.

The party went on gaily. Everybody was friendly towards A; the captain in particular never stopped joking with her and saying how glad he would be of her company on the voyage. A had no idea of the time, though it seemed to her that it must be getting late. As soon as she emptied her glass it was at once filled up again. Perhaps this was why she hardly noticed the others drifting away one by one until she suddenly realized that she was alone with the captain whose mouth was just opening in a gigantic yawn. Ashamed of having stayed for so long, A jumped to her feet. Presumably it was the liquor that made her feel all at once stupid and dazed so that she hardly knew what she was doing there with the yawning, alcoholic captain in the stuffy cabin full of smoke and cigarette ends and dirty glasses. She did not know the time; she did not know whether the boat had started to move; she did not even know the way to her own berth. Standing there stupidly like that she must

have wondered what in the world had come over her to make her
forget her precarious position and behave in such an imprudent way:
at the very start of the voyage, too, when heaven knows what serious
consequences might follow.

This was the moment at which the door started to open and someone came into the cabin. In her stupefied state A could not at first
remember where she had seen that round face and light moustache.
All at once it dawned on her that they belonged to the official whom
she had first interviewed, the one who had been so helpful and
friendly. But how could it be he? What could he be doing here
when all the officials had left the different departments long ago and
were at home with their families? It seemed to be the same man
and yet A was not absolutely certain. The official — if it really was
the official — had altered his appearance by putting on a heavy,
shapeless sort of a raincoat that almost reached to the ground, and he
was wearing besides a hat with a soft brim pulled well over his face.
He did not take off his hat although it was sodden with rain, but
looked silently, and as A thought, critically, from A herself to the
captain who seemed to be falling asleep on a narrow settee fixed
against the wall. For her part, A was too flabbergasted to do anything but gape foolishly until the newcomer abruptly stepped over
to her and said, I'm afraid you won't be able to sail after all. There
has been a hitch.

What sort of a hitch? Can't anything be done to put it right? A
wanted to know. But the other, instead of answering, merely told
her that she would have to collect her luggage and get off the ship
at once. At once: Do you understand? was the last thing he said,
looking keenly at A from the shadow of the dark hat brim, just
before he went out of the door.

If one is to analyse the affair it is extremely important to get an
exact picture of the official's behaviour, to know the precise tone
in which he spoke, and so on. But unfortunately A's impressions
are inadequate. All she repeats in response to questioning is that the
man did not seem angry or hostile and that he didn't take up a con-
demnatory attitude. His voice, apparently, was rather cold and
emphatic; quite different from his cordial way of talking earlier in

the day. But this might be expected from anyone called out late at night, in the rain, on a disagreeable errand. The question arises in one's mind, naturally, as to why the official — if indeed that was who it was — should take this task on himself instead of delegating it to one of his subordinates. At once, and with the added support of A's own uncertainty, one begins to doubt the identity of the messenger. On the other hand, we know that the authorities do often act in astonishing and incomprehensible ways, attaching the highest importance to matters which we think trivial, and vice versa. It appears to me injudicious to draw any conclusion from the data available.

The official's departure seems to have roused the captain, for as soon as the other man was out of the cabin he started up from his doze and asked what had been going on. A began to explain, but before she'd spoken more than a few words the captain impatiently interrupted her, just as if he'd really heard everything for himself, and in a boasting, blustering sort of way told her to pay no attention to what had happened but to stay where she was. Even in the midst of her dismay and confusion A thought this conduct very odd, and it made an unfavourable impression on her so that she wondered if the old man could have been shamming drowsiness for his own ends. With this suspicion added to everything else she was in a great hurry to get away. It seemed to her that after her original ill-advised behaviour every minute she spent on the ship now must be jeopardizing her position with the authorities still further. Without really listening to the other's noisy arguments she unceremoniously wished him good-bye and hurried out into a passage which was quite dark except for the tiny gleam of a blue bulb further along. A hadn't the faintest idea which way to go so it was lucky for her that the cabin door behind her opened again, lighting up the companion-way and her suitcase lying at the bottom of it just as she had left it when she first came on board. Her one idea now was to get ashore as quickly as possible. She did not even glance at the captain who, blocking up most of the doorway with his bulk, was bombastically advising her to do as he said, and repeating, with a queer mixture of aggressiveness and persuasion, that A had better sail while she had the chance. A did not answer him, but simply snatched up her suitcase and ran for the steps. The old man's voice followed her for a few seconds; it sounded either threatening or derisive, she wasn't sure which. As she reached the deck she heard a door bang and then everything became silent.

There were no lights showing anywhere on the ship, but a faint luminosity came from the sky so that it was just possible for A to see where she was going. A few lonely looking lamps were spaced at long intervals down the quay and near them various dark surfaces could be seen glistening with the fine rain that was persistently falling. The tall policeman had gone although the gangway was still in position: the whole place was deserted. Standing on the quay, A looked back at the black silent hulk she had just left. She was struck by the complete absence of movement or light: a ship on the point of sailing ought surely to be a scene of bustle, but here there was no sign of life. It seems that a notion came to her then that perhaps the ship had never been really intended to sail that night; perhaps it would not sail at all; perhaps it was not even a real ship, but one of those dummy ships which one sometimes sees used as waterside restaurants at holiday resorts. When the official had pointed it out from his window it had looked real enough. But how could A be sure that it was not some other ship she had seen from the window?

Preoccupied with these thoughts she walked the whole length of the quay without meeting a single soul. High solid gates barred the exit, and, as she approached, a policeman came out of a sort of guardroom on the left, flashing a torch which lighted up the falling raindrops like sparks. A recognized him as one of the men who had admitted her earlier on, and for an instant this seemed a good omen; but then she thought it might be unfortunate.

A had been through a wearing time and she has described the sense of deep exhaustion that came over her as she began to tell the policeman what had occurred. Now it seemed to her that whole days must have passed since she had been to bed; she felt as if she were almost falling asleep on her feet; and her voice, too, sounded, she thought, like someone talking in his sleep. She didn't look in the man's face as she was speaking, but past him, at the door of the guardroom which was ajar and beyond which firelight flickered and several people seemed to be moving about.

So you must open the gate and let me go out again into the town, she finished up: but she wasn't at all surprised when the other refused to do anything of the kind. Indeed, she would have been more surprised if the man had agreed, her own voice sounded so sleepy and unconvincing.

You can't go out, the policeman said in rather a truculent way. Your papers have been stamped and officially you've left the country.

But you see, that's really absurd, A replied mildly.

Without any impatience she repeated everything she had said before. This time her words seemed to make more impression because the policeman, instead of giving a flat refusal, muttered something about consulting some officer and stumped back into the guardroom again.

A did not in the least resent being left standing there in the rain. She felt quite apathetic, resigned to everything, even to her own weariness. With rain dripping off her hat she stood staring at the guardroom door which was now so nearly shut that only a thin golden streak outlined three sides of it. It must be nice and snug inside there, she thought (just as if some peaceful domestic haven were behind the door), just as a child thinks, without taking the thought any further.

Voices rose and fell indistinguishably inside the guardroom. A began to imagine that time must have stopped and that she was fated to stand for ever, with her suitcase beside her on the wet paving stones, exactly as she stood now. Then the door was pushed wide open. This time it was not the policeman who came out but a man wearing a soft hat pulled well over his face. A started out of her lethargy for a second. But after all, she thought, anybody would pull his hat down on such a wet night — she had done so herself — and besides this man was of much slighter build than the other.

She stepped forward, prepared to recite her piece for the third time, but the stranger lifted his hand in a silencing gesture. She could not see his face at all but she felt herself being scrutinized closely.

Apparently the man was satisfied with what he saw, for he presently turned round and re-entered the guardroom without having said a word; and in a minute or two the policeman came out, scowling into the rain, and hastily unfastened the gate. Too tired to speak, A picked up her suitcase and stumbled outside. Just as the gate was closing she took one last look along the quay towards the ship she had left. Perhaps even now at the last minute she expected to see the vessel ablaze with light, with sailors shouting to one another and running about: but it was all dark and still as the grave. To-morrow everything will be straightened out, was her final thought as she fell like a log on to the bed in a cheap travellers' hotel which luckily was still open near by. But probably she didn't believe this even then.

If A had ever seriously imagined that her affairs would be quickly arranged, her hopes must have vanished next day as soon as she entered the department on the third floor. The clerks who yesterday had received her so courteously, this morning seemed to have been waiting with quite different feelings for her to appear, and her arrival was the signal for a general outburst of suppressed giggling and choking and grimacing and leg-slapping. No sooner had she shut the door after her than the chief clerk got up from his desk and came up with a half mincing, half strutting gait that was intentionally provocative. He was a dark, frizzy haired, fancily dressed young man who looked as though he had native blood in him.

So you didn't get away after all, he said, leaning on the wooden barrier and staring at A insolently out of his prominent brown eyes. The two of them were so close together that A had an excellent view of his white shantung tie printed with a palm-leaf design. The opening phrase had evidently been prearranged, for the other clerks stopped their antics and sat silently goggling.

I want to see the head of the department as soon as possible, A said. She knew that to show any sign of irritation would simply delay matters so she forced herself to speak peaceably. Please let him know that I'm here. It's urgent.

You're in a great hurry all at once, aren't you? the chief clerk remarked. He pulled a pencil out of the bush of black hair over his ear and tapped it against his front teeth in a specially annoying way, never taking his eyes off A's face. Now that you've condescended to turn up, he added.

The fact was that A had overslept after her exhausting experiences on the previous day; nobody had called her, and it was now getting on towards noon. However, she didn't see any need to explain this to the chief clerk, so she merely replied that she had come as soon as she could.

What made you change your mind at the last moment about sailing? asked the young man. He made no attempt to move, but, as A didn't answer, suddenly adopted an openly sneering attitude. I suppose you lost your nerve and couldn't take it when it came to the point.

Luckily A had enough restraint to control herself. She knew that to start bandying words with the clerks was the worst mistake she could make, and that if she once allowed herself to be drawn into an altercation she might never get beyond the outer office at all. As she came in she had happened to notice an old newspaper lying on the bench provided for people waiting for interviews. Turning away now in disgust, she sat down, unfolded the crumpled paper, and held it wide open in front of her. The paper screened her from the clerks' impudent faces even though it couldn't shut out the noises they made. The whole office had begun to indulge in puerile jeering and joking at her expense. Seeing that A didn't show fight but remained inscrutable behind her newspaper the taunts grew louder and ruder. She's yellow; Got cold feet; Hasn't got what it takes; Quitter; Rat, were some of the gibes she was forced to listen to, accompanied by subdued catcalls, boos, hisses and other offensive sounds.

This was just the sort of situation that the clerks in our official departments always delight in, and of course they were determined to make the most of it. Like the rest of their kind, they derived the keenest amusement from mocking a poor victim who happened to be at their mercy. They're all the same, the clerks in these offices, an irresponsible, spiteful, childish, scatterbrained crew. One wonders why on earth the authorities put up with them. But not only is their mischievous conduct countenanced by their superiors, but it's as if they were actually encouraged in it: in fact, it almost seems to be one of the official requirements. I've often noticed how, when a well-behaved lad enters such a department, his whole character changes immediately; he loses his good manners, neglects his family, becomes flighty, quarrelsome and malicious, and spends all his spare time swaggering about with his fellows. Perhaps the clerks aren't really bad at heart but simply spoilt, thoughtless and conceited. No doubt they do work very hard at times — the enormous mass of official documentation witnesses to that — and the sedentary indoor life impairs their health to a certain extent. But when one has made allowance for these facts it's still difficult to see why they should be privileged to abuse their position as they do and to torment unfortunate people who have quite enough troubles to bear already.

A sensibly sat absolutely still, realizing that, just like children, the clerks would tire of their tricks before long if they didn't succeed in getting a rise out of her. Sure enough, after a few minutes, the baiting died down to disappointed mumbles, she heard someone go into the inner office, and presently the head clerk sulkily announced that the official would see her. Her last glimpse as she went into the other room was of a craning head and a pair of sharp eyes peering after her from behind every desk.

The inner office looked exactly the same as on the previous day with the holland blinds over the windows admitting a diffused light. The official was writing, he did not look up at once, and A studied him carefully as she came into the room. Yes, it was the same man who had come aboard the ship, there couldn't be any doubt about it, although he certainly looked different now in his smart office suit, and without his hat his face seemed younger and fuller. No, there couldn't be two people so alike, A was thinking, when the official suddenly pushed aside his papers and snapped out, Well, what do you want now?

Although she had expected to be met with coolness and possibly with censure, A was not prepared for such an uncompromising tone. She hardly knew how to reply. The other did not help her out at all, but confronted her with a cold, piercing gaze that was anything but encouraging.

I've come to find out what I'm to do now, she said hesitantly.

It appears that you've taken matters into your own hands, the official said in the same barking voice.

I don't understand, faltered A.

The man let this pass in silence and glanced at his watch. A realized with horror that she had created a bad impression by not showing up earlier. Worse still, it must be the time when the official went out to lunch so that the interview was likely to end before anything had been settled.

But you must be able to give me some advice, she began hurriedly. Surely you can tell me what I'm to do to put things right so that I can sail on another ship.

There won't be another ship for a very long time, the official said in the detached, final tone in which a person refers to a matter already disposed of. He seemed to be on the point of dismissing A who stood in front of him with a dismayed face; but he changed his mind and went on: You can hardly expect another golden opportunity of that sort. I've never known anyone offered a better chance.

Do you mean that I ought to have stayed on the ship, then? she exclaimed, completely taken aback.

You had a chance in a million.

A stared at him dumbfounded, trying to read in his round, expressionless face the correct interpretation of the last remark which, so it seemed to her, could be taken in two quite different ways.

But it was you yourself who told me to go ashore at once, she said slowly, after a pause.

The official turned his head and gave her a sharp look. For a second she thought he was going to deny ever having been on the ship, and the treacherous doubt plagued her again: What if I was mistaken? But the other, instead of settling the question once and for all, left her as much in the dark as ever by saying, Didn't the captain tell you to stop on board?

A admitted that this was true. She was about to continue that she had obeyed what she naturally took for the higher authority, when the official looked at his watch again and got up, remarking in an indifferent voice, Haven't you ever been told that a captain is always master aboard his ship?

For heaven's sake don't send me away already, A implored him. You must give me some help. Or if you won't help me yourself at least tell me who I'm to go to.

In her desperation she began following the official about the room while he, hardly seeming to have heard her, was putting some papers into a brief-case and getting his hat and overcoat out of a cupboard. What am I to say to the home authorities? A asked despairingly.

That's up to you, the official said, struggling into his coat which seemed to be rather tight in the sleeves. He spoke in a casual, abstracted way as if he had lost interest in the whole affair and was already thinking about something else. We have no contact here with any other authorities, he added in the same bored tone. His attitude towards A had changed altogether and was now merely impersonal and offhand as though he were seeing her for the first time. Of course, you could try the other departments, he went on, rapidly slipping one button after another into the buttonholes down the front of his overcoat: But, frankly, I don't think it would be much good. In any case, there's nothing more I can do. But you're quite free to take whatever steps you like on your own account.

A says that if she had fully realized what lay behind those words she would have thrown up the sponge there and then. Yes, she once told me mournfully, I would have done better to have thrown myself into the sea then. And when I think what people in her position have to go through I'm almost inclined to agree with her. What sort of a life is it when all one's time is spent in running from one department to another, forced to entrust one's fate to callous, feather-brained underlings who know perfectly well that they are dealing with an under-privileged person and probably never even trouble to put one's carefully prepared statements before their superiors? What sort of a life is it to live month after month in a hired room, with one's luggage packed, in case one should be summoned away at a moment's notice? What sort of a life is it to be alternately buoyed up or cast down by contradictory rumours, all equally unreliable and ephemeral, or by an imaginary glance of encouragement or disapproval from some passing official? What sort of a life is it to ponder for hours over the construction of a single sentence in still another appeal, which, if wrongly worded, might prejudice the whole case against one? What sort of a life is it when one is continually impelled to write letter after letter, doomed either to remain unanswered, or to elicit a new bunch of complicated forms or an incomprehensible official rigmarole which one studies feverishly and vainly in search of enlightenment?

Just imagine what it's like to be always risking humiliation by trying to ingratiate oneself with this or that petty clerk or hanger-on who might let fall a crumb of information. Just imagine the loneliness (for of course it's impossible to make friends in these circumstances even if there were opportunities of doing so); the monotony (for one can't concentrate either on work or amusement); the strain (for one never dares to relax for a minute for fear of missing some vital pointer).

Yes, it's a hard and mysterious system under which we live, and we can't hope to understand it. Whether or not there really exist laws governing official procedure is immaterial since it is impossible to investigate these secret matters. Perhaps the most incomprehensible thing of all is that a well-meaning person like A is as liable to heavy penalties as the worst criminal. Although we don't know what originally brought A under official notice I can say from my own knowledge of her that it couldn't have been anything you or I would consider a serious offence. And her second offence, if that lay in leaving the ship, was surely not much more than an error committed with the best intentions. I'm not defending the fact that she joined in the drinking party; obviously, to keep a clear head should have been the first care of a person in her predicament: and most likely all her subsequent misfortunes stemmed from that lack of restraint. Yet even here one sees extenuating circumstances. To begin with, she was already excited and over-tired when she arrived on the boat: and she was in a totally strange environment besides, in circumstances that were very difficult and disturbing. It would not have been easy for her to avoid taking part in the captain's celebrations or to have refused the drinks that were offered to her without

seeming unsociable or straitlaced. Yet for these actions she is condemned to do penance for many years; perhaps even for the whole
of the rest of her life. For who knows whether, although she achieved
her return long ago, the authorities will ever see fit to terminate her
protracted sentence?

A CERTAIN EXPERIENCE

ONCE, a very long time ago, an extraordinary thing happened to me. A very long time ago, I've written: but mere words can't describe the enormous stretches of time which have intervened between that incident and the present day. When I look back on it it's like contemplating something in a former existence of which one has miraculously retained memory. If I were a believer in the transmigration of souls, I should really be inclined to think that it did take place in an earlier incarnation. It has that remote quality; and at the same time it continues to exercise an obscure and profound influence over me, even now.

There are times when I hardly remember the occurrence at all. For quite long periods the memory seems to withdraw itself, to go into retreat, as it were. When this happens I become restless, and the great bird which always hovers above me swoops lower and fills my head with the stridence of his black wing-beats. At first, because the memory has really gone a little away, the cause of my uneasiness is not clear; I'll put it down to the oppressive weather, or perhaps to something I've eaten. But sooner or later a glimpse comes to me, as if, in the secret room where it had hidden itself, the memory lifted a corner of the curtain and peeped out of the window. Then at once I hurry off in pursuit. From that instant of realization my whole life becomes oriented towards the one objective of recapture. I feel like the owner of some beloved and valuable animal that has been stolen; or the parent of a kidnapped child. I can't rest until the precious memory is safely housed again in my consciousness.

What was this wonderful event? someone may ask sceptically. It certainly must have been something unique that happened all that time ago and is still so important that you can't bear to forget about it. Anybody can say that they've had a mystical experience without fear of contradiction because there's no way of proving the matter. But surely this is something more definite. Describe it to us. Tell us about it.

Well, the experience did have its objective aspect which can be described in quite simple language that anyone can understand. For instance, it can be stated plainly that I was condemned, that I was imprisoned, that I had given up hope, and that I was then delivered and set free without stipulations. I can describe the courtyard with its high spiked walls, where shuffling, indistinguishable gangs swept the leaves which the guards always re-scattered to be swept again. I can describe the peep-hole in the hookless door, the hard, unsleeping eye-bulb in its cage. I can describe the smells in corridors, the sounds ambiguously interpreted, the sights from which eyes were averted hastily. I can describe the hands under which I suffered; I can describe the visitor with the rolled umbrella who announced my release.

But all these descriptions, no matter how detailed, give only the bare shell of the experience, the true significance of which beats within them like a heart that can never die. The objective side of the matter does in fact die; or at least it can be said to grow old and desiccated and frail as a beetle's discarded carapace. But the mysterious and private heart never ceases to beat. Indestructible and immortal, the heart beats on, independent, and beating for me alone. It's the personal nature of the experience which is incommunicable and which gives it its supreme value. What does it matter if the outward manifestation withers and shrivels and ultimately even crumbles to dust as long as the priceless heart still survives? Perhaps I was mistaken in the gentleman who spoke with such smooth reassurance. Perhaps I was taken in by the umbrella encased slim as a wand in its black silk tube. To judge from what happened afterwards it seems likely that I was too trusting on that far-distant occasion. Nevertheless, painful and ruinous appearances cannot kill the heart of the experience which continually beats for me; no less strongly in the shadow of threatening wings.

BENJO

It's true that I've never talked much about the things that happened to me in the other country. When my friend used to ask me questions about my life over there I found it hard, impossible almost, to answer: and now I find it equally hard to explain why this was so. It wasn't, as he assumed, simply that I'd forgotten about it. I don't deny that my memory is bad. My recollection of that far-off time as a whole is incomplete and blurred, there are a great many gaps and inconsistencies in it, and the chronology is inexplicably confused. On the other hand, I can remember a number of disconnected episodes quite clearly; I could certainly have related them to him if I hadn't felt so reluctant to break the shell of privacy in which they were encased. For a long time it was as if a sort of tabu were laid on the whole subject of my experiences abroad. It was the greatest effort to me to focus my attention on that period at all because, as soon as I started to concentrate, I used to be overcome by something I can only describe as a mental blackout. And this wasn't because the memory was unpleasant to dwell upon. Quite the reverse, the impression that always remained with me of those days was of a wonderfully tranquil and happy time. No, I can't really account at all for the inhibition that persistently kept me silent so long, nor for its gradual weakening. Now that no one questions me any more about these affairs I am able to contemplate them without interference. The curious thing is that now that no question-induced blackout obscures them, the memories themselves seem to be evaporating. The curtain which used to cover the picture has been removed; but now the colours of the paints are starting to fade. Every day the canvas becomes more indistinct, a ghostly landscape, with a few figures, such as Benjo's, appearing here and there, still touched with the bizarre gleam of their original brightness.

I hadn't been long in the country when I first made Benjo's acquaintance. By the way, I never discovered whether Benjo was his surname, or an abbreviation, or just a nickname: he was always referred to simply as Benjo. It was early in the morning when I first saw him. I know I hadn't been long in the old house I had bought, because the men who had been at work on the renovations had left only a few days before. The place was intended for a farm-stead, but for some reason the land had been sold off separately while the building remained empty for several years. You couldn't have called it a good buy from the practical standpoint: the house was dilapidated and old-fashioned and inconvenient, and very isolated and inaccessible too; but the price was low and I wasn't deterred by the drawbacks, numerous as they were. The thing that really appealed to me about the property was its situation high up on a lonely hillside with a wonderful sweeping vista of chestnut forest and a distant view of the sea. There was a rough little hamlet of grey, primitive cottages about half a mile away, but it was hidden by a fold of the hills. All you could see from my windows was the wild garden where anemones and red tulips grew in between the stones, and then the great cascading fall of woods to the sea.

The early mornings there were often specially beautiful, and this particular morning I'm thinking of was one of the best. It was very still — the wind didn't usually rise till about ten o'clock — and the islands seemed to be floating light as cloud-castles just above the horizon. After all the dreadful anxiety I'd been through I felt that I could never absorb enough of the peace, the beauty, the solitude; and so I wasn't altogether pleased to see someone coming along the track that led to the garden gate. At first I thought it might be one of the workmen who had mislaid something, a screwdriver perhaps, or a scarf, and was coming back to see if he'd left it lying about any-where. However, I soon saw that it wasn't a workman who was strolling towards me, but somebody I'd never set eyes on, a sur-prising figure in that out-of-the-way place, a big, tall, heavy man, smartly and rather eccentrically dressed in light trousers and a canary-coloured pullover and a white linen cap like a yachting cap with a long peak. I stood at the window wondering who could be visiting me at this early hour. It was really rather annoying; I hadn't even had breakfast yet and the kettle was just on the boil.

I had a vague idea that if the stranger saw no one about he might go away, and instead of showing myself I just stood where I was, watching him. His behaviour was as eccentric as his appearance, for instead of coming up to knock at the door as anyone else would have done, he began wandering about the garden with his hands in his pockets, looking at the house and surveying it from all sides with his head tilted and his eyes screwed up like an artist criticizing a sketch. After several minutes of this, having thoroughly scrutinized the house from every angle, he approached the door with the same rambling, indolent gait. By this time my curiosity was aroused and I at once let him in. He greeted me by name (but without introducing himself), took off his cap, dropped it on to a chair, shook my hand, and began to congratulate me warmly on the improvements I had made to the property. All this seemed very odd. I was certain I'd never met the man before and yet he spoke as if we were old friends. In my bewilderment I stared hard at him, trying to place his full, florid face which had a curious softness and shapelessness about it like a baby's face, or like an unfinished model in plasticine.

Benjo. How can I give the clearest picture of him? I think the word which best describes his whole personality is one which I've used already about his fashion of walking, the word 'indolent'. Yes, everything about him seemed heavy and lazy, like a great, sleepy, good-natured tame bear. Just like a bear, too, in spite of his friendliness, there was something a little bit sly and suspicious about him, although you couldn't say what it was. His face was so soft and plump, like a happy baby's; and yet the little eyes, the pink, incomplete-looking mouth, were not quite reliable. These impressions I received at the start although they didn't become crystallized until later on. At that first meeting I was impressed most by his friendly attitude which was really very engaging. And when the kettle boiled over in the kitchen and he urged me not to delay my breakfast, I invited him to share it with me.

While I was making the tea and putting the breakfast things on a tray my visitor remained in the living-room. Through the open door I could see him lounging about the room and looking at everything with his screwed-up eyes just as he had done outside the house. It rather irritated me to see him do this; but then, as soon as I came in with the tray, he began complimenting me on my good taste, admiring my books and the arrangement of the furniture, in such a simple, jolly way that I was placated at once.

The idea occurred to me while we were eating that he might have lived in the house himself at one time, or had some connection with the previous owners which would account for his interest, and I asked him if this were the case. Oh no, he replied, I've thought about living here often enough, but I didn't want to take on the job of doing up the place.

I wondered just what he meant by this. He didn't look as if he were short of money. His clothes, though far too ostentatious for my taste, were well made and of fine quality, the brilliant pullover was of softest wool embroidered on the pocket with an unknown coat-of-arms. No, I decided, it probably wasn't lack of funds but sheer slackness that made him fight shy of embarking on renovations.

The mysterious embroidery ornamenting his pocket stimulated my curiosity about him. Several times I was on the point of asking his name, but I was restrained by shyness and by my ignorance of the country's social conventions. In view of the friendly way he was treating me I felt it would appear a discourtesy on my part to inquire who he was. We sat there over our teacups for quite a while. My companion had a lazily humorous way of talking about local matters that was entertaining if not without a streak of malice. He seemed to have an intimate knowledge of everything that went on, and I asked him if he had lived in the district a long time. I come and go, you know, was his drawling answer to this: come and go. And then he ponderously heaved himself up from his chair and prepared to depart. Come and see me whenever you feel inclined, he said as he was leaving. Just ask for Benjo — anyone will show you the way. As he went off smiling to himself I realized that I still hadn't any idea why he had visited me: unless perhaps he had just looked in to inspect the place and see what I had done to it.

Outside the gate he passed the old woman who came from the village each day to clean up for me, and paused to say something to her which brought a wry grin to her rather sour old face. So Benjo has been to see you already, she remarked as she came in and began taking off the big black straw hat, shaped like a basket, that she wore tied under her chin with two shabby ribbons. At the time I thought she was referring to the early hour, but afterwards I wondered whether another significance lay at the back of her words. I would have liked to question her about the remarkable Benjo who was evidently well known to her (how could such a conspicuous figure fail to be well known in an isolated village?), but I don't approve of gossiping with servants and she herself had nothing more to say although several times during the morning I caught her glancing at me with rather a queer expression. I always found the inhabitants of that remote district very insular and reserved; a fact which emphasized by contrast Benjo's geniality.

One afternoon a few days later I decided to pay my return call on him, and stopped to ask my way at the combined post office and inn in the centre of the village. It was a depressing place, dark as a cave and full of some rank, unclassifiable smell, but in spite of its unprepossessingness there were always three of four yokels hanging about there; I suppose because they had nowhere else to meet. These idlers seemed to find something amusing in my request to be directed to Benjo's house. One fellow who had such a hairy face that he might have changed heads with an Ainu burst into loud laughter, exclaiming, She asks us for Benjo's house! She asks! But the proprietor came up and silenced him with what I thought unnecessary roughness, pushing him angrily to one side, and, accompanying me for a few steps, pointed out with his pipe the road I would have to follow. You can't miss it, he said. Just make for those black trees you can see there against the sky. I thanked him, and he nodded his head once or twice in the dour way they have in those parts, before he went back to the others who were watching from the dark mouth of the door.

It only took me a few minutes to walk to the group of firs which showed up conspicuously against the predominant bright green of the chestnut woods. There was no sign of any sort of a dwelling; only a narrow, crazy track that might have been made by rabbits, looping and faltering between the crowded tree-trunks. This trail soon led me to a small clearing in the middle of the plantation. But here there was nothing to be seen either, except what looked like an old weatherbeaten gipsy caravan derelict under the trees. I was just going to turn back to the road when, to my amazement, the upper part of Benjo himself suddenly emerged through the window of the caravan, like a very large snail protruding from a very small shell.

So you found your way here, he called out cheerfully. And how do you like my country residence? He waited for me to approach, laughing as if the whole thing were an excellent joke, and leaning out of the narrow window in which he had the appearance of being tightly wedged. Come up: you'll find it very snug, he went on. But as I put my foot on the lowest of the four steps that led to the door at the back of the caravan, he seemed to alter his mind, saying, Perhaps it's really a bit cramped for the two of us inside, and on such a fine afternoon we'd do better out of doors.

Next moment he opened the door and brought out two folding chairs which he passed to me down the steps. If you'll just take these I'll see if I can find some refreshments, he said. Through the little door I could only get a glimpse of the interior of the caravan littered with books and papers amongst which Benjo's enormous figure was rummaging. Then he came out with some glasses and bottles of beer and the door was banged shut.

I seem to have given you a surprise, he said while the chairs were set up on the slippery brown floor of pine needles. He kept laughing as he poured out the beer, and I could see he was very much tickled by my astonishment.

But is this where you really live? I asked in the stupid way that one falls into when one's thoroughly taken aback. I don't know what sort of a house I'd expected Benjo to have; probably some showy villa in keeping with his style of dress. I noticed that he was just as spick-and-span in his gaudy way as at our previous meeting, and I wondered how he managed to look so dandified when he lived like a gipsy. There didn't seem any room for his clothes or anywhere to keep them in the caravan. And what was the meaning of all those books and papers? Benjo was the last person I should have suspected of studious habits. Could he be conducting some kind of private business out here in the woods? I began to realize then what a dark horse the fellow was.

I come and go, he said, just as he'd said it before. Here to-day and gone to-morrow, you know. Then, as if he guessed my doubts and wanted to banish them, he became serious and went on in a very reasonable tone, Of course, it has its drawbacks, it's not luxurious, it's by no means all that I could wish. But on the other hand there are definite advantages in this style of living. It's cheap and healthy, and convenient for getting about, and I'm able to get through a lot more work than I would if I were living somewhere where people were continually dropping in on me and distracting my attention.

I didn't know what to think. There was certainly something queer and inexplicable about Benjo; and at the same time he was so naïf and so anxious to be friendly that it seemed unworthy and even absurd to distrust him. After all, he was more like a big, clumsy, harmless, friendly animal than a man, lolling back there in his seat with a drowsy, good-natured grin. Most likely there was some quite simple explanation of his odd idiosyncrasies.

I stopped with him until we had finished the beer, but without getting a second chance of looking inside the caravan. Feeling that I'd already been guilty of rudeness in displaying so openly my surprise at his living arrangements, I didn't like to ask any questions. Benjo himself did not refer again to his mysterious 'work': nor did he again mention his domicile until, just as I was leaving, he remarked, Now you can see why I envy you your cosy quarters up there on the hill.

I've described this interview with Benjo in some detail because, in its way, it was typical of my whole association with him. I suppose 'association' is the right word to use about a relationship which always continued superficially cordial without ever remotely approaching intimacy and without ever losing (on my side) a faint element of uneasiness. In spite of my longing for solitude there were days when loneliness overcame me in the strange country and I was glad to see Benjo's massive form loafing along in some garish costume. At other times I would be irritated by him almost

unbearably, or filled with a vague, amorphous suspicion that even
bordered upon alarm. Living alone in a lonely place one's few
human contacts assume disproportionate importance, and so
Benjo occupied a larger place in my mind than was warranted by
the actual time that we spent together. How often did we see one
another? I have the impression that at some periods we met
frequently, almost daily. At other times weeks would go by
between our encounters. Quite often Benjo would leave the
village, and for days on end his caravan would be missing from the
clearing among the pines. When this happened, I believe that I
experienced a lightening, a sense of relief, of which, however, I
myself was hardly aware. Yet I was not displeased when, after a
solitary spell, I heard that he had returned. It was almost invariably
the old cleaning woman who first gave me the news. Benjo came back
last night, she would announce while she was fetching a broom from
the corner or starting to wash up the breakfast dishes. Or, Benjo
will be with us again before sundown. I didn't ask her, though I
often wanted to, how she obtained this information about his
movements which she never failed to pass on in a portentous voice
as if it had some special personal significance for me.

Looking back now, it seems to have been Benjo who visited me
far more often than I visited him. In fact, I can't really be certain
that I went again more than once or twice to the caravan or that
I ever got another glimpse of its interior. Probably one of the
reasons for this was that in order to get to the fir plantation one
had to walk through the village, and I always avoided the place as
much as I could. There was something indefinably depressing to
me about the grey little houses and their uncompromising inhabitants. Benjo, on the contrary, was quite at home in the village
where he spent a good deal of time drinking and gossiping at the
inn, apparently on excellent terms with the habitués. From there
it was an easy walk for him to my house, and he acquired the habit
of strolling up the hill with a bottle of beer which we would divide
between us. His behaviour towards me was always precisely the
same. The same lazy, jolly, bantering manner; the same flippant,
slightly malicious talk about this trifle or that; the same indolent

way of slouching round, hands in pockets and head tilted to one side, staring at everything in sight. As time went on this trick of his got on my nerves more and more acutely. My irritation reached such a pitch that I could hardly restrain myself from bursting out in protest at his inquisitive attitude. Yet all the time I was bothered by the feeling that my annoyance was unjustifiable. Why should I resent a person taking a friendly interest in my activities? Everything I did seemed to interest Benjo, whether I was gardening or working indoors, painting a cupboard or putting up shelves or some such odd job in the way of making the place more comfortable. He would lounge near me for hours, not helping actively, but encouraging me with appreciation and sometimes with suggestions of his own, and all the while smiling with the sort of complacent expression that might be worn by a landlord who watches a good tenant improving his property.

When winter came on I expected to see less of him. The winters aren't very severe in that district, but the high winds and heavy rainstorms are quite enough to make a camper's life unattractive. Benjo, however, continued to come and go as usual, although he grumbled about his hardships whenever we met. I simply couldn't understand the man's conduct. His clothes were as expensive and ostentatious as ever, he seemed to have money to burn, for I heard stories of how he would turn up at the inn with his pockets stuffed full of notes and coins and stand treat to the whole village. Why on earth didn't he take himself off to some reasonable dwelling?

But he merely came to my house more frequently on the pretext that his own quarters were so miserable. He made himself very much at home, dropping in at all hours, and almost behaving as if he had some right to be there. I can't explain how it was exactly, but he began to adopt a sort of proprietorial attitude that was inexpressibly aggravating and also somehow disquieting. Once or twice when I came back from a walk I found that he had climbed in through a window and was sitting in front of the fire, and I'm certain that he'd been snooping about the place in my absence. Nothing seemed to have been moved, there was no proof that he'd touched anything; and yet I had the feeling that everything in the house had been closely examined. On another occasion, coming in quietly from the kitchen, I actually caught him peeping through my bedroom door which he had surreptitiously opened. Over and over again I'd tell myself I was a fool to suspect him of anything worse than childish curiosity: wasn't he just as simple and mannerless as a great boobyish boy? Or I would try to think of him as some foolish, unwieldy, well-meaning animal that had attached itself to me and hadn't the sense to realize that it wasn't unreservedly welcome. But all the same I was often uneasy now in his presence, I would feel a nervous antipathy towards him whenever I heard his heavy, dawdling steps that advanced so inexorably to my door.

One day I actually asked him point blank why he didn't buy or rent a decent home of his own. You can be sure I would have done that by now, he answered, if this place of yours hadn't spoilt me for anywhere else. It's a mistake moving into a house in a hurry. Much the best plan is to wait until you find somewhere that really suits you.

You'll have to wait a long time if you're wanting this house, I said, because I've got no intention of leaving.

That was the moment, when we both laughed as if at a joke, that my buried intuition of what was coming took its first step towards consciousness.

In all this time I've never really been able to make up my mind about Benjo. Did he really know that I should be summoned away so soon, so finally, and in such lamentable circumstances? Sometimes I still incline to the idea that he was just a simpleton who played his part accidentally, or, at the worst, was merely an unconscious tool. At other times the weight of evidence seems to cast him for a far more sinister role. His plentiful supply of ready cash, his sudden arrivals and equally abrupt disappearances, the inexplicable presence in his caravan of all those papers and books, even the detail of the embroidered crest he so frequently wore; all these things can be taken as pointers towards some official connection. But against this one is obliged to consider his characteristic laziness, which surely was not assumed and which was quite incompatible with authority: and his doglike quality of friendliness, which, though it could be tiresome enough, was genuinely disarming. I find it hard to believe that he was aware all the time of what was going to happen: but looking at the other side, I find it hard *not* to believe. However, it's unprofitable to puzzle one's head over these old questions, which now, in any case, no longer seem very important. What I feel now is nothing sharper than a perplexed and melancholy regret when I think that all the time it was for Benjo that I worked away at the house where I was not permitted to reside, and that perhaps to-day Benjo's unappreciative eyes are watching the islands I never visited float like castles on the remote horizon.

NOW I KNOW WHERE MY PLACE IS

VERY soon after I arrived in the southland I began hearing about the hotel. I don't mean that it was notorious in any way, it was never mentioned in the sensational press like some of the gambling places and so-called country clubs, but somehow or other its name always seemed to be cropping up. Like everybody else the friends with whom I was staying spent a good deal of time swimming and playing tennis, and while I was with them on the beach or perhaps walking off the courts after a game, I would hear someone near by casually mention that they had lunched at the hotel the previous day or that they were going to dance there that evening.

Curiously enough, it was never one of my own friends who made a remark about the hotel. In fact, in some obscure way which I don't attempt to explain, I got the impression that they deliberately refrained from referring to it in my presence, that they would actually have preferred me to remain unaware of the proximity of the place.

Of course, when I first heard it mentioned it meant nothing more to me than a name; it might just have been any southern hotel that was being discussed. But is that the exact truth? Looking back now from this distance of time it seems to me that even then, on that very first occasion when a girl in a green swimming suit, strolling along the beach and swinging a straw hat in her hand, spoke about the hotel to her companion as they passed; even then, in the level and unequivocal shore light, something stirred in me, the little hyacinth that blooms inside my heart quietly unfurled a new petal.

Was it really the same place that they were talking about? The place that for so many years lingered like a half memory on the horizons of my consciousness? How often through the slow school terms, and afterwards when life conducted me into quite different situations, did the tenuous picture appear before me in that vague twilight between sleep and waking! How well my imagination was acquainted with the peculiar tower, rounded like the keep of

an innocuous fairy-tale stronghold. How intimately I seemed to
have experienced those balconies, those light-crowns in the great
hall, those tropical gardens with their palms and flowering shrubs
and tall beds of succulent cannas. All these things I had been
accustomed to accept as part of the queer dream-plasma which
flows along like a sub-life, contemporaneous with but completely
independent of the main current of one's existence.

Did I ever really visit the hotel when I was a child? You may
think it strange that I am in doubt about such a simple question.
But life is so uncertain these days, everything that happens makes
me more and more unsure of myself or of anything else, so that I
really can't speak positively about events that took place so long
ago. Practically each day one is confronted by some manifestation
of precariousness, some proof of the unreliability of one's judgment
and senses, so that it becomes impossible to make a definite statement about anything that one sees or hears. And if this is true of
contemporary happenings how much truer it is of things belonging
to the remote past which are in any case subject to distortion
through the mere accumulation of hours. Why, I could cite endless
examples of deceptive appearances, of perplexing, dubious and
enigmatic events, inexplicable and disturbing discrepancies by which
one is continuously surrounded and with which one is expected to
cope, heaven knows how.

One seems to be living in a perpetual fog; and it's because of all
this obscurity that I feel in doubt about the hotel. Perhaps I did sit,
a small, serious and rather lonely figure with straight fair hair, under
the electric brilliance of those enormous crowns illuminating the
dining-hall. Perhaps I did occupy myself with mysterious and
solitary pursuits, too grave to come into the category of games,
among the speary cannas that towered over my head like a fabulous
jungle growth bursting aloft into an orange and vermilion fire.

Or perhaps it was really only a picture of the hotel that I saw in
an album of photographs at my old home. I remember so well the
album bound in some very soft leather and embroidered in coloured
beads with an Indian symbol. Is it really the soft roughness of the
leather, not unlike velvet, that comes back to me along with the

slim elegance of satinwood furniture and the stippled scentless rain of hydrangeas? Or is this, too, just an illusion and the blue-tinted photograph, round which constellations seem to be wheeling, no more than a shadow in an old dream?

I'm no nearer to knowing the answers to these questions than I was when I first saw in one of the southern shops a postcard with a picture of the hotel. The sight on the prosaic card of that curious rounded tower had a violent effect on me. I immediately made up my mind to visit the place and at the first opportunity I asked my friends to drive me there in their car. At first they hesitated, disconcerted, I could see, by my direct request, and displaying the same unaccountable resistance that I had previously noticed in regard to their attitude towards the hotel.

At last I persuaded them to do as I asked. It would have been difficult for them to refuse without actual rudeness for I was not to be shaken in any way from my determination.

An afternoon was decided upon for the expedition and we set out. I was excited and gay. My companions, as if making the best of a bad job, now that they were irrevocably committed to the undertaking, started off cheerfully enough. But as the drive continued their mood changed: long pauses punctuated the talk and it seemed to me that I could detect in their manner and in the looks which they exchanged traces of reluctance and even of anxiety. When I tried to discover the reason for their disquietude, asking them if they disliked the hotel, if it were too expensive, if the road to it were bad and so on, they returned evasive replies, forced themselves to talk carelessly for a while, but soon lapsed into silence.

Gradually I myself became infected by their uneasiness. The look of the landscape, too, through which we were travelling was not reassuring. For some time after leaving the town we had been driving across a flat, parched, yellowish plain, uninhabited apparently, and useless as pasturage, for the short lion-coloured grass was brittle and dry and no trees gave their shade. A range of low mountains sullenly barred the earth from the sky which was now invaded by strange upright clouds as by a battalion of ominous ghosts.

The way must have been longer than we anticipated as the day was fading into a thundery half-light when we reached the narrow peninsula at the end of which the hotel was situated. Here there was nothing on either side of the road but a few sand dunes patterned with coarse grass and beyond that the two vast expanses of calm and uncoloured water. We drove for what seemed a long time along this road before we reached the hotel. The monotonous lava-grey continuity of sky and sea exercised a hypnotic effect on the eye. All existence seemed to have dwindled to that one narrow, monotone and trance-like progression between languidly droning seas.

How can I describe the dramatic way in which the appearance of our destination broke into this tedious entrancement? Suddenly the evening mists cleared away, a pure, cool light, not sunshine, but the aftermath of the sunset glow, filled the western sky and touched the long backs of the waves with an ethereal radiance. A million luminous scales shimmered on the breast of the little harbour where yachts were moored. The hotel stood on higher ground overlooking the harbour. Many of its windows were already lighted, and as I gazed at the strange rounded bulk of the tower a flock of large birds in wedge formation flew very high above it towards the west.

I got out of the car and hurried up the steep incline in front of the building. My friends tried to detain me, calling out that they wanted to look at the harbour while some daylight still remained, but I paid no attention.

Perhaps it would have been better if I had waited for them and we had gone all together up to the hotel, the ramifications of which, not lofty, but rambling and spacious and decked out with creepers and balconies, reminded me of one of Genji's summer palaces.

But would it have made any difference after all? Would the presence of other people have deterred the small figure with straight fair hair who gravely approached me between beds of cannas that twilight had already deprived of their colours? And after all, why should I deny her? In this world of false friends and dangerous ambiguities where nothing is what it seems, isn't it best to accept whatever comes without resistance or inquiry, relying only upon the unassailable knowledge that in one's heart a hyacinth is secretly and inviolably blooming?

OUR CITY

'I did believe, and do still, that the end of our city will be
in Fire and Brimstone from above.'

I

How often one hears our city spoken of as 'cruel'. In fact, this
adjective is used so frequently that in many people's minds cruelty
has become accepted as the city's most typical and outstanding
attribute: whereas there are in existence a great variety of other
qualities, probably equally characteristic and certainly just as
remarkable.

To my mind, one of the most astonishing things about the city
is its plurality. In my own personal experience, for example, it
has, during a comparatively short space of time, displayed three
distinct manifestations of its complex being. And if it is possible
for one individual in one brief period to witness three such changes,
just imagine the astronomical number of different forms in which
our city is bound to appear through the centuries to the millions of
its inhabitants.

In my case, the first metamorphosis was, I think, the most un-
expected; for who, even among the unprejudiced, would expect the
city to show itself as an octopus? yet that is exactly what happened.
Slowly, with deliberation, and at the same time as it seemed
almost languidly, a blackish tentacle was unfurled which travelled
undeviatingly across the globe to the remote antipodean island
where I imagined myself secure. I shall not forget the tentacle's
deceptive semi-transparency, something like that dark Swedish
glass which contains tints both purple and black while still keeping
translucence. The tentacle had the same insubstantial, ethereal
look: but it had also a strength many times greater than that of the
strongest steel.

The second metamorphosis was, by comparison with the first,
almost predictible. It was, in a sense, logical, and though I won't

go so far as to say that I actually anticipated it, I certainly recognized its inevitability when it appeared. As a matter of fact I believe I really did, if not consciously or completely, at least in some obscure, inchoate way, foresee it; although it's difficult to be quite sure of this after the event. We all of us know from films or pictures or the posters of the Society for the Prevention of Cruelty to Animals, those hideous toothed traps, sadistic jaws which snap upon the delicate leg or paw of some soft-furred wild creature, mangling the flesh and splintering the fragile bones and clamping the victim to a slow, agonizing death. There is even a sort of resemblance between the serrated blade as it must appear shearing down on its prey and the ferocious skyline of a city partially laid waste.

With regard to the third metamorphosis, I am in an uncertain position. To me this aspect of the city's character, though less clearly in sequence than the second, still is quite comprehensible and far from surprising in view of what had gone before. But to an outsider, someone from another part of the world, I can see that it may well seem the most astonishing manifestation of all. 'How can a city be a judge at one and the same time?' I can imagine such a man asking: 'a judge, what's more, who not only arraigns the criminal, sets up the court, conducts the trial, and passes sentence, but actually sees that the sentence is carried out.'

To such a person I can only reply that I have no explanation to give him. These things are not well understood, and doubtless there's some good reason why we don't understand them. The most satisfactory attitude is to accept the facts as they are without too much probing, perhaps simultaneously working out some private thesis of one's own to account for them.

No, I can't explain how our city can be at one time a judge, at another a trap, at another an octopus. Nor have I any way of elucidating the sentence passed on me, which is really two sentences, mutually exclusive but running concurrently: the sentence of banishment from the city and of imprisonment in it. You may wonder how I have the heart to keep on at all in such a hopeless position. Indeed there often are times when I'm practically in despair, when the contradiction seems too bitter and senseless and incomprehensible to be borne. All that keeps me going then, I think, is the hope that some time or other I may by chance come upon the solution, that one half of the contradiction will somehow dissolve into the other, or the sentence as a whole be modified or even remitted. It's no good approaching these obscure matters systematically. All one can do is to go on living, if possible, and moving a little, tentatively, as occasion offers, first in one direction and then in another. Like that a solution may ultimately be found, as in the case of those puzzles made of wires intertwined, which suddenly and by a purely accidental manipulation fall apart into two halves.

II

There's a street near where I live which is very ugly. It's not a slum street but part of what is called a respectable, cheap neighbourhood. The people who live there are quite poor. The refugee woman who works in the library rents a room in this street. She has taken refuge there. I should have thought myself that it was more a place to escape from.

It's not only the small, yellowish-grey houses which are ugly: the actual roadway that pitches not steeply uphill, the lamp-posts, the squat air-raid shelter, even the gutters, all seem to have an air of meanness and malevolence which is frightening. The street has a smell, too. It is, as far as I can describe it, a sour smell, with spite in it. A smell of asphalt, of dustbins not emptied often enough, and spite. The people who walk in the street look spiteful too; they glance at you resentfully as they pass, as if they would like to do you an injury. They look at you as if they wished you were at their mercy. I should hate to be handed over to the mercy of the people in this street. Even the children who dart up and down have faces like spiteful gnomes. A little girl in a plaid dress pushes past me, her limp, uncombed hair brushes my arm, and that moment, from just underneath my elbow, she lets out a shrill screech that pierces the whole afternoon. I feel as if a hobgoblin had jabbed a long pin through my ear.

The bald, excrescent shelter which I'm now passing has a curious

morbid look, like some kind of tumour that has stopped being painful and hardened into a static, permanent lump. It reminds me of
one of those chronic swellings you sometimes see on a person's
neck which has been there so long that no one but a stranger notices
it any more. The entrance to the shelter is screened with wire
netting. I look through. The inside of the place is unclean.

Now, something quite extraordinary occurs in the street. A small
dog comes round the corner, running after his mistress. Yes, actually
a dog; what a relief. And what's more it's a dog of that particular
aristocratic, antique breed, half lion, half marmoset, from which,
rather than from any other species, I would choose a companion if
ever again it became possible for me to know such happiness as
companionship with a dog.

This little dog, coloured like a red squirrel, runs with the gay
abandonment peculiar to his race, his plumy tail streaming behind
and seeming to beat the pavement to the rhythm of his elastic and
bounding movements. How can I explain my emotion at the sight
of that small, heraldic-looking beast careering so buoyantly? The
appearance of these dogs when they run has always seemed to me
quite amazingly intrepid and lively, at the same time both brave
and amusing — even faintly absurd — yet somehow exceedingly
dashing and debonnaire, almost heroic, in the style of diminutive
Quixotes launching themselves without the least hesitation upon the
enormously dangerous world.

The lion-dog runs forward with all his racial gallantry and *élan*,
into that ugly street smelling of asphalt, sourness and spite. It comes
to this, then, as I see it. One must try to live up to the dog's standard.
That's what one must aim at.

III

How blue the sky is this morning: as if summer had kindly
approved the date set for putting the clocks on another hour. It's
only the fourth of April and now we've already got double summer-
time. To-day might easily have been foggy like it was most of last
week; it might have been pouring with rain, or blowing a gale, there

might even have been a snowstorm. But, thank goodness, the weather is perfect. There isn't so much to be thankful for these days; the people walking uphill to the candle-spired church must often be hard put to it to find suitable subjects for thanksgiving in their prayers. To-day, though, everybody can thank God for the fine weather. And people with gardens, how happy they must be: they've got an extra cause to give thanks with the daffodils springing bright everywhere and the blossom coming out on the fruit trees just as prettily as it does in countries which are at peace. Overnight, as it seems, the chestnut buds have burst into harmless miniature flares, beautifully green. All the trees which have been dull and dormant so long are now suddenly lit up by these miraculous green fires, gentle beacons of hope, quietly and graciously burning. Oh, how blue the sky is. The barrage balloons look foolish and rather gay, like flocks of silver-paper kites riding high up there in the blue.

In the garden of the small house below the church an old cherry tree is just on the point of blooming. Thousands of tiny white buds, still close and firm, tremble all over the branches among golden-green leaves the size of a mouse's ear. On some of the upper boughs, more exposed to the sun, the blossom is out already, and here the open petals cluster so thickly that it looks as if snow showers had caught and lingered among the young leaves. A few early bees have found out the cherry tree and are working busily over the white flowers.

The foreign girl who lives in the little house leans out of the window. She's quite close to the cherry blossom, she could almost touch the starry sprays if she leaned out a little further. A brightness comes on her face, reflected perhaps from the bloom. Or perhaps the humming bees and the twittering of the birds remind her of home. Perhaps she suddenly remembers hearing those cheerful sounds under a stronger sun.

The girl is in no hurry to leave the window. For quite a long time she leans out with her arms on the sill, and the wind lightly stirs the fair hair beside her face which in spite of its bright look somehow gives an impression of sadness. From where she stands she can see over the garden wall into the street of grey quiet houses leading uphill to the church. It is the hour of the morning when in ordinary times the church bells would be ringing. There are no bells now, and the few people on their way to the service walk slowly, separated from one another, in dark clothes that look too heavy for the spring day. At the open door of the house opposite a woman and a little boy are watching the people disappear one by one into the church. When the last one is out of sight the mother puts her hand on the child's head, turns him gently back into the house with her and closes the door behind them without a sound.

The street is quite empty now under the blue sky across which a cloud in the shape of a swan is airily floating.

In a moment a girl comes round the corner, walking fast. She is dark-eyed, very slender, and well dressed; her high heels tap merrily as she hurries along. She sees her friend at the window, waves to her, and calls out a greeting. The foreign girl runs down to meet her, and soon they are sitting on the grass where a sprinkle of white petals has yet to fall. How happy they seem together under the cherry tree, talking, and smiling often: the dark eyes gleam in the sun, the grey eyes reflect the tender blue of the sky. The dark girl gives news of her husband, a soldier fighting far off in the desert, from whom she has just had a letter. While she speaks of him her face is lively and beautiful. The foreigner leans forward with eagerness, rejoicing in her friend's pleasure.

Something catches her attention so that she turns her head. Look, a butterfly, she calls out. The first butterfly of the year. The first one I've seen since I left my home.

And then, as she watches the wavering flight of the pretty red-brown butterfly, the animation dies out of her face, her eyes lose their blueness and slowly darken with tears. The other girl, too, becomes grave, the words she is saying falter, dead before they are spoken, the fragile happiness which these two had nourished between them vanishes like the butterfly whose uncertain, frail wings seem to be at the mercy of the first breath of wind.

It is not only the exile whose cheeks have become wet: and though they are both conscious of this they say nothing about it, they don't speak of anything sad, but quickly start talking about some clouds which are coming up shaped, not like swans, but like small shying horses. Soon both the girls are smiling often again. Probably it's only an illusion that their voices no longer sound quite so gay. Out-of-doors, in the lovely spring weather, how could anyone help feeling gay? So beautifully blue the sky is; the cherry blossom so white.

IV

The clock by my bed has a dial that shines in the dark. It is a small white clock with a shutter which slides over its face when it starts out on a journey. This clock has accompanied me on many tremendous journeys. It has been stowed carefully away and muffled against damage in the gales of northern oceans; the spray of tropical seas has tarnished its metal parts; from beside many beds it has patiently watched with me the solemn march of the constellations of two hemispheres.

Now it stands with the same patience at this improbable city bedside. It ticks in the same unflurried, impersonal fashion. Its tick does not sound either friendly or unfriendly: it has a sound which suggests impartiality. It is an impartial, scientific observer, this clock, quietly recording into eternity all that passes in front of its face. In spite of our long association, the clock and I are not on intimate terms; my feeling for the clock is one of respect more than cordiality.

Just now the hands of the clock stand at half-past two. They gleam greenishly in the dark. I've been asleep for an hour. A minute or so ticks away. Then there is noise. The sirens wail up and down my room with howling violence. It always happens like that, it's always the same, it's not the sirens that wake me: I always wake up a minute or two before the alert actually sounds. The siren noise comes to an end: other noises begin. Mobile guns grind elephantinely over me. A plane buzzes round my head. Outside the black windows the searchlights climb questing. I can feel the broad beams sawing and the narrow beams scissoring through my nerves. Then suddenly from far away over the city, dull, muffled, heavy noise. Pandemonium is starting up; is coming nearer and nearer, implacably; is here, ultimately, on top of me. The darkness explodes into thunderous tumult. Through it all I catch the slither of some small object falling inside my room. I put out my hand to the switch, and, incredible as it seems, the light goes on just as usual. In the calm yellow light I see that it is, of course, the picture on the chest-of-drawers that has slipped on the polished wood and fallen down on its face. It always happens like that, every time it's the same, the vibration always makes the picture fall down. The noise batters the night with unappeasable fury. The whole night outside is rent and rocking in all directions. I cover my ears in a vain attempt to shut out some of the din; in particular, there's one excruciating sound which resembles, magnified to the nth degree, the screech of tearing canvas that I desperately try to exclude.

The noise makes me feel inexpressibly lonely. I am quite alone in the little house, alone with the clock whose tick I can no longer distinguish. I have the impression that I'm the only living soul in the midst of this fiendish hullaballoo. Can there really be other human beings out there in the city? Impossible to imagine that people are connected in any way with the racket that's going on. It's an absolutely inhuman excess of noise, the rage of the city itself. Our city itself is ravening at the night.

Like a lighted bubble my room floats irresponsibly in the shattering noise. The curtains flutter a little, but the pale blue carpet doesn't turn a hair. It's a fact, the pale blue carpet actually still covers the floor from wall to wall. The din seems incessant, but there must be infinitesimal pauses, for at some moment I am aware of the clock ticking attentively. I hear the bottles on the dressing-table snigger against one another. Ages go past like this.

At last things grow quieter: the noise is diminishing, retreating, petering out. Planes snarl frantically overhead, then zoom off, away from the city. Someone walks quickly along the street outside with heavy steps: a warden, perhaps. So there are people alive, moving about in the city. The clock goes on ticking, a diligent and indefatigable recorder. Presently the all-clear sounds, interminably, like a boy seeing how long he can hold his breath. At last even that noise stops; and there is immeasurable relief. Very carefully, being as quiet as possible, I switch out the light.

The noise is over. But now something begins to happen that is in its way as sensational, as appalling. Through the darkness of the blacked-out windows I am aware of an indescribable movement throughout the city, a soundless spinning of motion in the streets and among the ruins, an unseen upward surge of building: the silence industriously, insecurely, building itself up. The silence gathers itself together in the parks and the squares and the gaps and the empty houses. Like a spider's web rapidly woven, the frail edifice mounts up quickly towards the moon. Soon the precarious work is finished, the whole city is roofed, covered in with silence, as if lying under a black cloche. The tension is frightful. With compressed lips and foreheads lined with anxiety every citizen crouches uneasily, peering up at the transparent black bell of silence hanging over our city. Is it going to break?

v

What a heartbreaking contrariness there is in this world. It seems as if things were deliberately, cunningly, planned to cause one the maximum amount of chagrin. Take this little house where I live now, for instance. What could be more inappropriate to a person in my predicament than these two pleasant rooms, one of which is actually carpeted in pale velvety blue? There's something shocking and painful in the mere thought of associating myself in my present unhappy state with anything so frivolous as a blue carpet. And yet there have been periods of my life when a place like this would have suited me perfectly. Then, of course, I was unable to find anything of the sort, and was forced to exist in some gloomy setting as out of keeping with my circumstances at the time as this cottage is with my present position.

I sometimes wonder what induces the authorities to allow me to stay here, in comfort, with pictures, with lamps. Probably it won't be permitted much longer. There have been indications lately that a change is contemplated. Who knows from what stony barrack, what freezing cell, I may before long find myself looking back on all this with nostalgic regret? Quite likely it's with that very object that I'm left here at present — just so that the change, when it comes, shall be all the more intolerable. O yes, they're ingenious enough for anything, those into whose hands we are committed.

Certainly it was a subtle finesse to decree that the first bitter months of my sentence should be served in an environment which continually seems to be making a mock of my sufferings with its incongruous gaiety. Often there are days now when I feel absolutely desperate, when the weight of my burden seems far too heavy to bear. And on these days the place takes a callous delight in flaunting itself, as if determined to draw my attention to the fact that not I but some happy, privileged being, perhaps a charming young actress with many lovers, really ought to be living here. The very pictures on the walls, portraying as they do light-hearted columbines and nymphs in amorous poses, smile down on me with cynical mockery.

The fact that the windows look out upon trees and gardens is part of the cruel design. For in this way I am sometimes tricked into forgetting the city; I fall into the trap of believing that I am free, that there is open country outside and not streets and ruins. And then comes the terrible moment when it occurs to me that the city is still there; and I pace from corner to corner, of course finding nothing, but still blindly searching for something that might not reject me, in the dreadful destitution of the condemned. How everything in the rooms jeers at me then. The walls shake with laughter. The painted houris sneer, curling their rosy lips at the idea that I should still be looking for mercy after all my misdeeds. Not even the sparrows that I've just fed with crumbs from the window restrain their ridicule, but fly away tittering. And the carpet, the blue carpet: the pale blue carpet finds it necessary to spread out its softness under my feet in sheerest derision.

It's queer that I can't get out of the way of walking about. Here in the city, where few people except eccentrics ever walk unless forced to do so, I still don't seem to be able to break this countrified habit. A part of the distance between the cottage in which I sleep and the place where I work is occupied by an area without houses, a stretch of heath or rough parkland, where children play and dogs run about sniffing the grass. Every afternoon, for some time now, I've walked across this stretch of land which is partly wooded and partly covered with thickets of gorse and bramble. There's a pleasant path here that runs through the trees. At a particular turn of the path a silver birch bends over it, as if shaking out a threadbare green curtain.

To-day it was cooler and darker than usual under the trees. I stopped in an open clearing and looked up at the sky. The segment that lay behind me, towards the west, was full of a limpid light; the part ahead darkened softly with blowing clouds. Chromium against gunmetal, the barrage balloons on which the light fell embossed themselves on the tarnished shield of the sky. And above them, much higher up, so high as to seem no larger than a migration of birds, a huge formation of bombers was steadily travelling towards its distant night-time objective. Sometimes blurred, sometimes flashing with brightness, the machines in outlandish beauty pursued their lonely and awful course, filling the whole atmosphere with a muted thunder.

Why was it so dark and chilly down in the wood? I thought at first that I must be later than usual. And then it suddenly dawned on me that this hour which up to now had been afternoon had to-day slipped over the boundary into evening, and that the brown, scorched look of the trees came, not from drought, but from approaching winter. In the thinning foliage, here and there certain yellow leaves trembled and said 'Death' with a frightened voice.

A nondescript, paunchy man sauntered through the wood, whistling to a black dog. Then two very ordinary middle-aged people came round the curve under the silver birch. The man wore

an officer's uniform, but was not at all martial looking: he held his
cap under the arm farther from his companion, and from the hand
at the end of this arm there dangled a string bag containing packages
and a bottle of milk. His hair was grey and quite thin; his tunic did
not fit very well and he seemed to sag a little at the knees as he
walked. The woman with him looked like a housekeeper in a shapeless fawn coat and a serviceable brown hat that had never been gay.
Quite suddenly and spontaneously these two people turned to one
another and linked hands and walked on swinging their joined
hands lightly and proudly between them, like young lovers. They
could not repress the timid joy in their faces, and smiled at everything that they passed, at me, at the dog, at the trees. I began to
make an effort to master myself as soon as I saw them, otherwise I
must have burst into tears or thrown myself on the ground or started
tearing my clothes with abandoned fingers. When one sees people
like this so happy it is hard indeed to endure one's sentence. Why,
even a paunchy, nondescript man has his black dog which accom-
panies him unquestioningly in faithful devotion wherever he
chooses to go.

VII

Our city is full of the troops of a foreign army. When I first
arrived here from the other side of the world I couldn't tell whether
these soldiers were friends or invaders, and even now I'm equally
at a loss.

Wherever money is being spent these men in their costly and
elegant uniforms are to be found, in theatres, bars, restaurants,
stores, buying the best of everything, and conducting themselves
in a lavish way far beyond the resources of the citizens who are
pushed quite into the background. Very often it's impossible to
get what one wants — whether it's a meal or a drink or a seat at an
entertainment or some article in a shop — because these people have
bought up everything. And as for taxis and cars — well, the drivers
seem to have placed their vehicles exclusively at the disposal of the
foreign soldiers and their bottomless purses.

Are they, in fact, allies or enemies? Often enough one hears bitter remarks which suggest the latter alternative. But if that were the case wouldn't the hostility of the citizens take some more dynamic form than mere acrimonious grumbling? And then, it must be admitted, the conduct of the strangers isn't what one traditionally expects of a conquering army. Beyond the fact of their ubiquitousness and the way in which they monopolize all amenities, they appear not to interfere with our city at all. They have not, for example, taken over control of any of the public services or made any attempt to alter the laws or impose their own restrictions.

Occasionally, though this doesn't often happen, one sees them going about with the local people, usually girls they've picked up somewhere, or perhaps a youngster impressed by their spending powers. Or one catches sight of a group of their high-ranking officers formally escorted by a party of our dignitaries through the doors of a solemn official building.

One's natural impulse, of course, is to question somebody and settle things once and for all. But a person in my situation can't be too careful; I have to think twice about whatever I do, even about such a simple thing as asking a question. The last thing I want is to draw attention to myself in any way. And then, with our complex system of regulations, continually changing from day to day, how is one to know what is permitted? If I were to make a mistake the result might be fatal for me. A single false step might easily end in disaster. Besides, even if I were so reckless as to stop a passer-by and make my inquiry, how can I be sure that he'd give me an answer? As likely as not he would merely look at me suspiciously and pass on, even if he did not actually lodge a complaint against me. For a passionate secretiveness characterizes the inhabitants of our city. It simply isn't worth while taking such a chance. I'd rather remain uncertain.

It's not as if the foreigners were constantly being brought to my notice, either: in the way I live now, I often pass two or three days without seeing a single one of them.

In the beginning it was quite different. Before I was directed to the work which now occupies me, while I had time on my hands to wander about the city, I naturally gave a good deal of attention to the strange soldiers whom I saw everywhere lounging about, apparently as idle as I was myself. In those days I had some peculiar notions about them. Laughable as it may seem, I developed the idea that these men were in some way linked to me, that there was something in common between us, like a distant blood relationship. I, the city's outcast and prisoner, seemed to feel with these foreigners a connection, sympathetic perhaps, which did not exist where the citizens were concerned. Often, as I glanced at the strangers, their large, tanned, dispassionate, ruminative faces would touch some recollection in me; I would suddenly be reminded of the faces of friends in a far-distant country, the conviction would sweep over me that I was here confronting members of a race that had once been most dear to me, like brothers. And this emotion was so strong that it was all I could do to restrain myself from making an appeal of some kind to them, in my desolation.

I remember particularly one such occasion. I was waiting for a bus in one of the main streets when my eyes wandered idly towards a foreign captain sitting at a small table outside a restaurant. Immediately the sensation I have described came over me, but with such intense poignancy that it was as if I had suddenly caught sight of a beloved and well-known face among the indifferent crowd. Instinctively, hardly knowing what I was doing, I started moving towards this man, some incoherent phrase already forming itself in my head. Heaven knows what I might have said to him, what fantastic supplication for comfort, for aid, I might have poured out to him. But, precisely at that moment, as if at a given signal, he got up in a leisurely manner and strolled away. It seemed to me that only a few yards separated us: that I had only to take one or two steps in order to catch up with him. And, crazily, I did start forward, meaning to overtake him. Perhaps he had entered one of the neighbouring shops; perhaps he had started to cross the street and was hidden by passing cars: in any case, he had already vanished completely. The pavement, as usual, was crowded with the strange uniforms, so much smarter and better fitting than ours; and for the next few moments I kept staring distractedly into one and then another of those unknown faces, some of which looked back at me I believe not unsympathetically. But not one of them was in the least like the face for which I was searching, and which I suppose. I am never to see again.

Perhaps it was lucky for me that I was denied the opportunity of speaking; but how can I be sure, having no means of obtaining information about the soldiers? So I must go on in uncertainty, even though foreign eyes still sometimes seem to gaze at me in passing with a look of fraternal compassion and understanding, encouraging me to do the thing which I most fear doing.

VIII

Like a recurrent dream, the following scene repetitiously unfolds itself: I am sitting in a bureau, putting forward my case; it is the nine-hundred-and-ninety-ninth station of my tedious calvary. In front of me stands the usual large desk covered with papers and telephones; this one has on it, too, a small notice, neatly printed and framed like a calendar, saying, 'If danger becomes imminent during an alert the bureau will be closed'. Behind the desk sits the usual bureaucrat; this time it's a big man with curly hair and a pin-stripe suit who confronts me discouragingly.

My voice goes on and on like a gramophone record. I'm not listening to it, I don't pay any attention to the words coming out of my mouth. The whole speech became mechanical ages ago, and drearily reels itself off without any assistance from me. Instead of associating myself with the dismal recitation, I stare out of the window from which it looks as if some destructive colossus had been stamping upon our city, trampling down whole blocks and boroughs with his gigantic jack-boots. Acres and acres of flattened rubble spread out spacious and so simplified that the eye is baffled and it's impossible to tell which objects are near and which are remote. It's not possible to say where the cheek of the earth starts to curve, or where the unsuppressed bright river loops over the bulge, down to the oceans and the archipelagoes on the underside of the world. The few buildings which remain intact in this vicinity stand about self-consciously amidst the harmonious demolition. They look singularly uncomfortable and as if they had taken fright at their own conspicuousness: one can see they do not quite recognize themselves in such embarrassing circumstances. They stand there at a loss, wishing to retire into the decent collective security which they dimly remember as being their proper place; or else to lose definition by amalgamating with the undetailed collapse all around them.

Just to the side of the window, a wing of the building from which I am looking juts out sharply at right angles, and here, on the roof and in the interior, I can see men repairing some damage it has sustained. From a gaping black tear in the wall a workman in shirtsleeves is starting to lower a bucket down the façade. I notice his face contracted in concentration, he's so close that I can distinguish the hairs on his arms which are straining away at the rope as he lowers the bucket with immense care, as if there were a baby inside it. What on earth has he got in the bucket? If only I could find that out perhaps everything would suddenly come right for me. While my lips automatically go on shaping the phrases of my petition, I am leaning forward and craning my neck in the hope of having a peep inside the bucket which is now hidden from me by the window-sill.

Suddenly I'm snatched away from my preoccupation by the angry voice of the bureaucrat, my own voice snaps off into startled silence in mid-sentence, as if the needle had abruptly been lifted off the record.

'What's the good of coming here with this rigmarole, wasting my time?' the man at the desk is exclaiming. 'Surely you know we don't deal with matters of that sort in my department — what you need is a public advisor — he's the person you ought to go to.'

'An advisor?' I repeat, in amazement: I can hardly believe my ears. 'Is someone in my position allowed to consult an advisor, then?'

For some reason my astonishment makes the bureaucrat still more indignant. He thumps the desk with his fist so that the telephones give a nervous, frustrated tinkle, the pens shake apprehensively in their tray.

'I've no patience with people like you,' he shouts rudely. 'How do you ever expect to get your affairs in order when you haven't got even enough sense to find out the proper procedure?'

He gets up and approaches me round the desk, and I hastily jump off my chair and back away from him in alarm.

'Be off with you!' he cries. His face is suffused with scarlet rage. If he were wearing an apron he would certainly flap it at me, but as it is he can only shoo me towards the door with his hands.

I retreat as fast as I can from the loud, angry voice and the red face bearing down on me threateningly. So it is that I never discover the contents of the bucket which, all the same, I associate with the bureaucrat's astounding suggestion.

IX

'And one has nothing and nobody, and one travels about the world with a trunk and a case of books, and really without curiosity. What sort of a life is it really: without a house, without inherited possessions, without dogs?'

Sometimes I think that the author of those words must have been under a sentence not unlike mine.

It may seem incredible that such a man, a writer of genius and famous into the bargain, could have been found guilty of any crime. But the hard and incomprehensible fact stands that the most frequent convictions and the heaviest sentences fall to the lot of just such sensitive, intelligent individuals as this very poet whose words have so much emotional significance for me. There is, I believe, a kind of telepathy between the condemned: a sort of intuitive recognition which can even make itself felt through the medium of the printed page. How else should I feel — without fear of appearing presumptuous, either — for this great man of another nation, this dead man whom I never saw and to whom I could not have spoken, the tender, wincing, pathetic solicitude that painfully comes into being only between fellow-sufferers?

How intimately I experience in my heart just what he must have felt in all of those unknown rooms, some of them poor, perhaps, and some splendid, but all opposing him with the cold fearful indifference of other people's belongings, against which he has to defend himself as best he can with his poor lonely trunk and his case of books.

And I — I haven't even a case of books to defend me. In my defence I can call up only the few volumes for which I was able to make room when the clothes and personal necessities had been packed into my trunk. They are honourable and precious to me, these books, in proportion to their great heroism. They are like members of a suicide squad who do not hesitate to engage the enormously superior enemy, life, upon my behalf.

When I start to think of my books individually it is always the same one which takes first place in my mind: the only one of the bodyguard about whose loyalty, so to speak, I have any doubt. I have had this book that I'm thinking of for a long time, and until just lately it has never been out of my keeping. I'm not sure how it reached me originally; whether it was a present, or whether I came across it by accident on some bookseller's shelves. I only know that the author's name was unfamiliar to me. I read it first during that fabulously remote period before my troubles began. I remember the horror the story inspired in me then, and how I wondered that any normal brain could conceive and elaborate so dreadful a theme.

But then, as things went from bad to worse with me, as my circumstances became more and more unpropitious, as I wandered further and further into the maze of misfortune from which I have never succeeded in extricating myself, then my feelings towards the book underwent a change.

How can I describe the profoundly disturbing suspicion that slowly grew upon me, for which at the start there was no sort of justification? Again and again I tried to rid myself of it. But like a latent venom it dwelt obstinately in my blood, poisoning me with the idea that the story told in the book related to myself, that I myself was identified in some obscure way with the principal character. Yes, in time it crystallized into this: the terrible book revealed itself as my manual, tracing the path I was doomed to tread, step by step, to the lamentable and shameful end.

If I had come to detest the book it would have been natural. If I had destroyed it or thrown it away one could have understood that. But instead, I developed a curious attachment to it, a dependence upon it which is very hard to explain. Of course there were times when I reacted against the book. On such occasions I felt convinced that it was the origin of my bad luck and that all the disasters which have overtaken me would never have happened had I not first read about them in its pages. But then, immediately afterwards, I would be eagerly turning those pages to discover what fresh tragic or humiliating or confusing experience was lying ahead of me.

This ambivalent attitude prevented me from coming to any hard and fast decision about the book: but whether I regarded it as an evil omen or as a talisman, it was always of the greatest significance to me and the idea of parting from it was unthinkable. I even felt uneasy if I was separated from it for more than a few hours. Particularly on those days which I expected to bring forth some new development in my case, a superstitious anxiety compelled me to carry the book everywhere I went.

That was how I came to be carrying it under my arm in the advisor's office. How I wish now that I had left it at home. But how could I possibly have guessed that I should be required to deposit some item of personal property there as a token? It came as the greatest surprise to me when, at the end of the interview, I was informed of this regulation. And why did this advisor select the book as a suitable object, drawing it from under my arm with a smile and putting it down on the top of a pile of other books on a writing desk in the corner? He might just as well have taken my scarf or one of my gloves or even my watch. I have wondered since then why I didn't make any protest. But at the time I allowed him to take the book from me without a word. I was too disconcerted to think clearly, and I was unsure of myself. I was afraid of prejudicing myself in the eyes of the man upon whose somewhat doubtful advice I was prepared to rely. Once he had taken the book in his curiously small, delicate hands it was too late to interfere.

But each time I go into the room and see it lying there, inaccessible although within easy reach, a conflict begins in my heart and I feel deeply disturbed. I start wondering whether my wisest course would not be to seize the book and carry it off, even at the cost of forgoing a support which, however dubious, is all that's left to me now.

X

My new adviser does not understand my case. There, now I have written the words I knew all the time I would have to write sooner or later. I am not surprised. Not at all. It would have been a thousand times more surprising if he, who is not even a native of our city, could have found his way through the enormously intricate labyrinth which a case that's been going on as long as mine has is bound to become. The thing which does surprise me is my own optimism. Surely I ought to recognize now that my number is up. Where do I always find enough courage for one more last hope? I am the enemy of this indestructible, pitiless hope which prolongs and intensifies all my pain. I would like to lay hold of hope and strangle it once and for all.

I have been to the adviser's office to-day. It is in a large building full of offices. To get to it from the street I had to walk up an alleyway between barbed wire and concrete-filled bins placed there to impede an attacking force. The officials who work in this building have a vast clientele. You can hardly pass through the alley without danger of being pushed into the barbed wire by one of the people who must hurry to get in or out of the place as quickly as possible. They are preoccupied individuals who frown incessantly, and the king himself would have to step briskly aside, if some abstracted client lost in anxiety took the notion of rushing past headlong to an appointment. It is noticeable that nearly all these impetuous, worried creatures are carrying brief cases of varying sizes which one can presume to contain the most urgent secret documents, the most dramatic dossiers. But I also saw commonplace people coming and going, little men with umbrellas hooked on their arms, and women with shopping bags full of parcels.

The waiting-room, when I finally got there, was crowded with people I seemed to have seen somewhere else. Yes, I already seemed to know all their faces only too well. When I had taken the vacant chair that might have been left purposely for me, I saw that among them, as they sat restlessly fidgeting, there were several boys and girls, school children, and some even younger. Although I'm not particularly fond of children I couldn't help pitying the poor little things, growing up in the vile atmosphere all these rooms have, impregnated with fear and suspense. What could they be but innocent at their early age? And what sort of future could be in store for lives beginning so inauspiciously? But the children themselves paid no attention to their environment. The youngest ones slept on their mother's laps. Some of the others leaned with empty faces against the knees or shoulders of grown-up people. Some were bored and made quiet overtures to each other to pass the time. A boy in a leather jacket had climbed on the window-sill; he had got his paper-white forehead pressed to the pane, and was gazing out at the sky as if saying good-bye to it. In a far corner of the room, two big men whose shoulders carried the words 'Heavy Rescue' had spread themselves out in chairs, and were staring dolefully at their huge black boots projecting in front of them. The air was stale, torpid, laden with unquiet breaths.

Meanwhile a constant bustle was going on in other parts of the building: one heard footsteps hurrying about, boards creaking, doors opening and closing, voices, raised sometimes in question or argument. Only we in the waiting-room seemed shut off from participation in the activity, like forgotten castaways wrecked in some stagnant lagoon.

From time to time the door opened a little way and an indistinctly-seen person peeped in and beckoned to one of the waiting clients who immediately jumped up and rushed out as if at the point of the bayonet. A stir of excitement went through the room each time this occurred, and it would be some minutes before those who were left behind settled down again to their restless vigil. I don't know how long this went on. I have the impression that hours passed, perhaps half a day. While I waited I remembered the important man who had been my advisor in former times; his elegant town house, his major-domo, the room with wine-coloured curtains where he used to receive me so promptly. The fact that I now had to seek advice in such a humble and undignified fashion brought home to me painfully how my affairs had changed for the worse. It was as if the authorities, by sending me here, had set their official seal on my degradation.

At last it was my turn to receive the mysterious summons. I had decided that when it came I would walk calmly across the room without impatience or flurry: but, just like everyone else, I found myself jumping up and making a dash for the door as if my life depended on getting through it at lightning speed. It was so dark in the corridor that I could only dimly distinguish a man's figure walking ahead of me with nonchalant steps. He opened a door on the left, signalled me to enter, and followed me in. Apparently it was the advisor himself who had come for me. He was a young, rather plump man, a foreigner obviously, with an impeccably-tied bow tie, and there was about him that finical, even dainty air which stout people sometimes have. It was the tie in particular which gave this effect, as if a neat, blue-spotted butterfly had alighted under his chin.

He stood fingering the ends of the bow delicately for a moment, smiling at me in a way that was both absent-minded and polite, before he invited me to sit down. I took the chair that he indicated and began to explain my case. The room was quite small and square, with green walls. Outside the window, almost touching the glass, was a large tree, still covered, in spite of the lateness of the season, with trembling green leaves. As the leaves stirred, watery shadows wavered over the ceiling and walls, so that one had the impression of being enclosed in a tank.

I felt singularly uncomfortable. My case was difficult to describe. I did not know where to start, or which particulars to relate, which to omit, since it was clearly impossible to mention every detail of the enormously protracted and complex business.

The young foreigner sat listening to me without making a single note. His manner was perfectly correct, but I somehow had the impression that he was not fully attentive. I wondered how much he understood of what I was saying: it was clear to me from the few words he had spoken that his grasp of the language was far from perfect. And why did he not write down at least some of the salient points of my statement? He surely didn't propose to rely purely on memory in such a complicated affair? Now and then he fingered the wings of his tie and smiled absently; but whether at me or at his own thoughts there was no way of knowing.

The situation suddenly appeared heartbreaking, futile, and I felt on the verge of tears. What was I doing here in this tank-like room, relating my private and piercing griefs to a smiling stranger who spoke in a different tongue? I thought I should stand up and go away, but I heard myself talking in agitation, begging him to realize the extreme gravity of my predicament and to give it more serious consideration, seeing that he was my last available source of assistance.

The young advisor smiled at me politely and made some vague fluttering movements with his small hands, at the same time saying a few words to the effect that my case was not really so exceptional as I thought; that it was, in fact, quite a common one. I protested that he must be mistaken, perhaps had not understood me completely. He smiled again, and repeated those indeterminate motions which possibly were intended to be reassuring but which only conveyed to me a distrustful sense of misapprehension. Then he glanced at his watch in a way that was meant to signify the end of the interview, and instructed me to come back again in two or three days.

I don't remember how I got out of the building: I've no recollection of passing between the coils of barbed wire in the alley. The sun was setting and I was in a residential part of the city that was strange to me; I walked up long, hilly, deserted streets between large houses, most of which seemed to be uninhabited. Dry autumnal weeds grew tall in the gardens, and the black window holes gaped with jagged fringes like mirror fragments in which the last rays of the sun stared at themselves bitterly. Then I passed a stranger who glanced coldly at me, and other strangers passed by with cold faces, and still other strangers. Armoured vehicles, eccentrically coloured, stood in an endless chain at the roadside, painted with cabalistic signs. But what these symbols meant I had no idea. I had no idea if there were a place anywhere to which I could go to escape from the strangeness, or what I could do to bear being a stranger in our strange city, or whether I should ever visit that stranger who was my advisor again.

**PETER OWEN
MODERN CLASSICS**

Since 1998 Peter Owen has been reissuing classic backlist fiction in the Peter Owen Modern Classics series. Currently numbering around ninety titles, the series brings together many of the greatest names from our six decades of publishing.

MODERN CLASSICS AUTHORS

Ryunosuke AKUTAGAWA, Li ANG, Guillaume APOLLINAIRE, Blaise CENDRARS, Marc CHAGALL, Jean COCTEAU, COLETTE, Machado de ASSIS, Lawrence DURRELL, Isabelle EBERHARDT, Shusaku ENDO, André GIDE, Jean GIONO, Alfred HAYES, Hermann HESSE, Anna KAVAN, Violette LEDUC, Yukio MISHIMA, Anaïs NIN, Boris PASTERNAK, Cesare PAVESE, Mervyn PEAKE, Marcel PROUST, Joseph ROTH, Cora SANDEL, Natsume SOSEKI, Gertrude STEIN, Bram STOKER, Tarjei VESAAS, Noel VIRTUE

Peter Owen Publishers
81 Ridge Road, London N8 9NP, UK
Tel: +44 (0)20 8350 1775 Fax: +44 (0)20 8340 9488
email: sales@peterowen.com

Trade orders:
Central Books, 99 Wallis Road, London E9 5LN, UK
Tel: +44 (0)845 458 9911 Fax: +44 (0)845 458 9912
email: orders@centralbooks.com

www.peterowen.com

Also published by Peter Owen

ICE
Anna Kavan

978-0-7206-1268-4 • 158 pp • £9.95 / / EPUB 978-0-7206-1415-2
KINDLE 978-0-7206-1416-9 / PDF 978-0-7206-1417-6
Peter Owen Modern Classic

'A classic, a vision of unremitting intensity
which combines some remarkable imaginative
writing with what amounts to a love-song to
the end of the world. Not a word is wasted,
not an image is out of place.'
– *Times Literary Supplement*

'One can only admire the strength
and courage of this visionary.' – *The Times*

'Few contemporary novelists could match
the intensity of her vision.' – J.G. Ballard

In this haunting and surreal novel, the narrator and a man
known as 'the warden' search for an elusive girl in a frozen,
seemingly post-nuclear, apocalyptic landscape. The country has
been invaded and is being governed by a secret organization.
There is destruction everywhere; great walls of ice overrun the
world. Together with the narrator, the reader is swept into a
hallucinatory quest for this strange and fragile creature with
albino hair. Acclaimed by Brian Aldiss on its publication in 1967
as the best science fiction book of the year, this extraordinary
and innovative novel has subsequently been recognized as a
major work of literature in any genre.

'There is nothing else like it . . . This *Ice* is not psychological ice or
metaphysical ice; here the loneliness of childhood has been
magicked into a physical reality as hallucinatory as the
Ancient Mariner's.' – Doris Lessing

Also published by Peter Owen

GUILTY
Anna Kavan

PB 978-0-7206-1268-4 • 158 pp • £9.95 / EPUB 978-0-7206-1441-1
KINDLE 978-0-7206-1442-8 / PDF 978-0-7206-1443-5

'Thrillingly unclassifiable' – *Guardian*

'A week after finishing *Guilty*, I'm still
haunted. Kavan's art is breathtaking – why
is there no *South Bank Show* on this genius
drug-fiend?'
– Duncan Fallowell, *Financial Times*

Not published until forty years after Anna Kavan's death, *Guilty*,
narrated by Mark, is set in an unspecified but eerily familiar time
and landscape. He begins the novel as a young boy whose father
has just returned from war. In spite of being garlanded as a hero,
Mark's father declares himself a pacifist and is immediately
reviled in a country still suffering from the divisions of conflict.
When his father is forced into exile Mark meets Mr Spector, a
shady figure who from then on is a dominant force in Mark's life,
seeing him through his schooling, employment and even finding
him accommodation. When Mark tries to break away from Mr
Spector to pursue an engagement with the beautiful but docile
Carla his life begins to unravel. Thwarted at every turn by a
Kafkaesque bureaucracy he begins to fall prey to the
machinations and insecurities of his guilt-ridden mind. Drawing
on many of Kavan's familiar themes, *Guilty* will be welcomed by
those who already know Kavan's work and a revelation to those
who don't.

SOME AUTHORS WE HAVE PUBLISHED

James Agee • Bella Akhmadulina • Tariq Ali • Kenneth Allsop • Alfred Andersch
Guillaume Apollinaire • Machado de Assis • Miguel Angel Asturias • Duke of Bedford
Oliver Bernard • Thomas Blackburn • Jane Bowles • Paul Bowles • Richard Bradford
Ilse, Countess von Bredow • Lenny Bruce • Finn Carling • Blaise Cendrars • Marc Chagall
Giorgio de Chirico • Uno Chiyo • Hugo Claus • Jean Cocteau • Albert Cohen
Colette • Ithell Colquhoun • Richard Corson • Benedetto Croce • Margaret Crosland
e.e. cummings • Stig Dalager • Salvador Dalí • Osamu Dazai • Anita Desai
Charles Dickens • Bernard Diederich • Fabián Dobles • William Donaldson
Autran Dourado • Yuri Druzhnikov • Lawrence Durrell • Isabelle Eberhardt
Sergei Eisenstein • Shusaku Endo • Erté • Knut Faldbakken • Ida Fink
Wolfgang George Fischer • Nicholas Freeling • Philip Freund • Carlo Emilio Gadda
Rhea Galanaki • Salvador Garmendia • Michel Gauquelin • André Gide
Natalia Ginzburg • Jean Giono • Geoffrey Gorer • William Goyen • Julien Gracq
Sue Grafton • Robert Graves • Angela Green • Julien Green • George Grosz
Barbara Hardy • H.D. • Rayner Heppenstall • David Herbert • Gustaw Herling
Hermann Hesse • Shere Hite • Stewart Home • Abdullah Hussein • King Hussein of Jordan
Ruth Inglis • Grace Ingoldby • Yasushi Inoue • Hans Henny Jahnn • Karl Jaspers
Takeshi Kaiko • Jaan Kaplinski • Anna Kavan • Yasunuri Kawabata • Nikos Kazantzakis
Orhan Kemal • Christer Kihlman • James Kirkup • Paul Klee • James Laughlin
Patricia Laurent • Violette Leduc • Lee Seung-U • Vernon Lee • József Lengyel
Robert Liddell • Francisco García Lorca • Moura Lympany • Dacia Maraini
Marcel Marceau • André Maurois • Henri Michaux • Henry Miller • Miranda Miller
Marga Minco • Yukio Mishima • Quim Monzó • Margaret Morris • Angus Wolfe Murray
Atle Næss • Gérard de Nerval • Anaïs Nin • Yoko Ono • Uri Orlev • Wendy Owen
Arto Paasilinna • Marco Pallis • Oscar Parland • Boris Pasternak • Cesare Pavese
Milorad Pavic • Octavio Paz • Mervyn Peake • Carlos Pedretti • Dame Margery Perham
Graciliano Ramos • Jeremy Reed • Rodrigo Rey Rosa • Joseph Roth • Ken Russell
Marquis de Sade • Cora Sandel • George Santayana • May Sarton • Jean-Paul Sartre
Ferdinand de Saussure • Gerald Scarfe • Albert Schweitzer • George Bernard Shaw
Isaac Bashevis Singer • Patwant Singh • Edith Sitwell • Suzanne St Albans • Stevie Smith
C.P. Snow • Bengt Söderbergh • Vladimir Soloukhin • Natsume Soseki • Muriel Spark
Gertrude Stein • Bram Stoker • August Strindberg • Rabindranath Tagore
Tambimuttu • Elisabeth Russell Taylor • Emma Tennant • Anne Tibble • Roland Topor
Miloš Urban • Anne Valery • Peter Vansittart • José J. Veiga • Tarjei Vesaas
Noel Virtue • Max Weber • Edith Wharton • William Carlos Williams • Phyllis Willmott
G. Peter Winnington • Monique Wittig • A.B. Yehoshua • Marguerite Young
Fakhar Zaman • Alexander Zinoviev • Emile Zola